About the Author

CU01506973

Michael Albert Capewell is a retired lecturer. His interests are computers, motorcycles, sailing and – of course science fiction. In his view, 'sci-fi' has played an important role in our development, providing targets for achievement in an entertaining, as well as a thought provoking way.........*sometimes!!*

Don't Touch Wood!

M.A. Capewell

Published by
THE OLD MUSEUM PRESS

Don't Touch Wood!

First published by The Old Museum Press Limited
The Old Museum, Bramber, West Sussex BN44 3WE
England
1997

© M.A. Capewell
All rights reserved

This book is sold subject to the condition that
It shall not, by way of trade or otherwise, be
lent, re-sold, hired out, or otherwise circulated
without the publisher's prior consent in any form
of binding or cover other than in which it is
published and without a similar condition
being imposed on the subsequent publisher.

A catalogue record of this book
is available from The British Library

ISBN 1 84042 011 1

Cover illustration, composition,
format and design by StewART

Printed and bound in Great Britain by
Biddles Limited, Guildford & Kings Lynn

Dedicated to my grandchildren, Nathan,
Ryan and Amber, to remind them of our frailty
in the nature of things and the need for friends,
from wherever they originate or
whatever they may look like.

A friend can change to an enemy, as in this story.
A stranger may be a friend.
Take nothing for granted, give everything a chance,
and by their fruits you will know them.
Oh, and yes, do touch wood.... very respectfully!

Chapter 1

It was a moonless night in September '95. Adam Briant gazed into a clear sky spangled with a tapestry of stars and planets - not knowing which was which - he wondered. That seemed to be the exact word to describe his feelings. He wondered not only about the difference but the enormity of his vision, and yet how small an entity he was by comparison. In fact the whole world seemed but as a speck of dust afloat in space and reality was not so different. Could life exist on other worlds? Would it be unique to earth? Is it not arrogant of man to consider himself the ultimate creation?

He came back down to earth with a jolt in surprise as Jenny his wife touched his arm and asked, "a penny for your thoughts."

"I don't need to charge you," said Adam "I'm sure you know, you usually do."

"Something to do with other worlds and secrets of the Universe if I know you, dreamer, maybe you should spend more time thinking about the problems down here on earth."

"You do that so much better than I do sweetheart, may I leave that to you?"

" As usual Adam, as usual," said Jenny reconciled to the fact.

It had long been a dream of Adam's to meet some day with a living entity from another world. There were so many other worlds in sight of the human eye, let alone those out of sight, that he considered the possibility of us being alone in the universe as frankly absurd. He also considered people who scoff at the idea, somewhat lacking intelligence rather than simply lacking in the vision and imagination that is so often attributed to people like Adam, by the kinder cynics that is. Vision and imagination he thought are the mark of all men and women of achievement throughout the ages, not something to be considered almost as an excuse by some people for the foolish considerations of someone that they feel needs some form of defence for his ravings. He reflected on the achievements of men of science many of who were inspired by writers of science fiction although they would not wish to acknowledge the fact. The rocketship, the laser beam (ray gun), journeys to the moon, and going further back the helicopter, the submarine, the armoured tank, organ transplants, etc. etc. These were all imagined by men of vision long before men of science alone, created them, almost one might say from their blueprints that rarely carried the copyright of their more materialistic mimics.

"Its getting a little chilly lets go indoors" said Jenny.

"Did you see that shooting star?" said Adam, "close your eyes and make a wish!"

Inside a log fire crackled in the fireplace and the inviting aroma of dinner drifted in from the kitchen.

"Smells good," said Adam, "I feel ravenous, stargazing always gives me an appetite."

The conversation over dinner was centred on the next day's work that included a trip into the City, which was Homer City, a place of large buildings and bustling crowds but quite an insignificant place of no great distinction, as yet! Adam had to buy supplies of wood for his furniture making business. He had a small business that employed five people making a variety of cabinets and chairs, quite flexible to customers' requirements as he had discovered was necessary to survive in a modern world. Adam found much satisfaction from working in wood, the natural warm feel had always appealed to him, his knowledge of wood types, grain working characteristics and even their heat producing ability when burnt, was quite extensive.

A feel for nature and a vivid imaginary ability or imagination, as others would put it which seems somehow a derogatory term. "Vivid imagination" seems like "a little loony." Adam appreciated the views of others but did not share their sentiments. In fact he was very thankful for this God-given gift even though it did cause some problems in his life. Problems with his personal relationships did result in anxiety both for himself and his wife when fact and imagination clashed but he still would not change with a person who would only consider proven facts as reality. He felt sorry for this type of person, and despised the type that poured scorn from their plentiful supply of ignorance. After all, if their way of thinking was correct, then reality would be static and the search for greater knowledge blighted. Is something only real when proven by man? He thought not. Almost as arrogant as the question posed by some. "Does a falling tree make a noise when no man is there to hear?" As though the absence of someone there to hear, alters the reality. The words of Jesus on the cross come to mind. "Father forgive them for they know not....".

This sort of questioning often passed through his mind and depressed him. Adam could not understand why educated intelligent men could not see beyond their own experience his own mind was so clear getting clearer as his eyes deteriorated with age. He could not see all the answers but he did perceive some of the questions unasked by many others. That is not to say that he considered himself unique or better than others, he knew there were people like himself, "dreamers" as they called them, and that it takes all sorts to make or destroy a world.

The evening meal finished, the couple relaxed in front of the television. The news was showing reports of murder trials, abuse cases and terrorist activities, all very depressing. However the final item (as though the good news had less importance than the bad) featured pictures from space; of distant areas where clouds of gas formed like some monster drifting in a great void. Amongst the clouds were newly formed stars from the furnace of creation and Adam's imagination started working overtime.

In this giant factory, stars were being created like some production line of creation. Stars that would have planets revolving around them and life, as we know it developed on some, and who knows what on others. Adam's mind went beyond this concept to the cause and or reason for this production and possible creator or creators. One God he thought but could all this be the work of one?

The enormity even swamped Adam's imagination and his reasoning failed, as he looked at the dog on the hearth taking in the pictures but unable to consider how the pictures were produced or even why.

He felt an affinity with his dog at that moment that he had not considered before, not many people viewing could either he thought. How little the majority knows or even care about the most important things in life he thought.

He then reflected on the diversity of subjects that people consider important; his teenage daughter's spots were the most important to her at the time, but priorities change and maybe in time the important things will attain something nearer to their true position in people's lives - whatever they may be.

He felt however that it would be an awful long time in coming. A second coming perhaps, or maybe we could ourselves become so Godlike as to not require such reverence of another form of life. Hopefully not he thought. Mankind would have to improve so much he could only consider the fact that they may think in their own minds that they could achieve such a state. The reality more likely not to be the case, but even now most scientists seem to revel in disproving a greater creation than mankind, striving, it seemed to him, to prove that man was already his own idea of God. He felt sorry for them or something close anyway. Adam knew what he thought about such men and wondered once more about our possible neighbours, as yet unknown!

The possibility of visiting another world is now history since the moon landing, but to visit another life-inhabited world seemed as far away as ever. In the physical sense it seemed extremely unlikely, due to the scientific discovery that not one of the planets in our solar system would support life as we know it. Either too cold, too hot, or poisonous gases, excessive gravity or other environmental problems. Life as we know it, as the saying goes, would be extremely unlikely. The possibility of life elsewhere in the universe however had to Adam's mind just taken on better odds with the discovery that other stars had been found to show evidence of possessing planets, something that he always knew somehow and therefore was not very surprised. To his mind the presence of other life was also inevitable. For one tiny speck of a world to be unique in the entire vastness was far too remote a possibility for him. Could they be aware of us? If a more intelligent life form did exist they may well know about us, he thought. Why have they not contacted us? Maybe they have, but not in such a way that their existence is recognised by the people as a whole.

Adam suddenly realised that Jenny was very quiet, in fact she had fallen asleep in her chair and the television was playing to itself. Occasionally, as Adam watched her, Jenny made movements in her sleep and murmurs of unrecognisable speech, she was obviously dreaming.

Adam considered the thought that ran through his mind. Jenny was in another state of existence, experiencing visions of reality but not reality itself, some of which she may remember when she awakened but possibly all will be forgotten. Her brain, like a computer wiping lost clusters of memory allowing her awakened mind to absorb more information without overloading or maybe assimilating experiences and knowledge. Who knows? He thought. Dreaming is still a little understood subject.

The dog too was in this state of suspended animation, his legs twitching in sympathy and Adam wondered if they may both be experiencing the same dream, a walk in the lane perhaps as they both often did. He woke them both gently. "Time for bed!" he exclaimed, "perchance to dream".

Chapter 2

The next day was bright and chilly and Adam rose at 7.00 a.m. as usual. After breakfast he prepared his pick-up ready for his trip into town. Charley, the dog, was already in the back of the pick-up ready to go, it was his custom to accompany Adam into town. Although he never was very keen on the traffic, he seemed to feel it was his duty to keep an eye on things and he did like to ride in the pick-up with his nose to the air-stream as the vehicle sped along, taking in all the sights sounds and smells. Minimum effort, maximum effect seemed to be his thoughts. Travel such as this was appreciated in a dog's way.

On another such occasion Charley had proved himself useful in warning Adam that a piece of timber had slipped through the pile and fallen off the pick-up into the road. As a result the timber was recovered before any harm was done. Adam had been especially careful since, considering the possible consequences he was glad to have Charley along on his trips either business or pleasure.

In town the timber suppliers were busy, but had Adam's order ready for collection due to the fact that he was a regular customer. They were used to his visits and as with all successful businesses, valued Adam as a customer.

Adam was grateful for this level of service, as he was able to make the round trip in half a day and be back home for lunch. An ordinary small business man going about his everyday business - but a man with someone else's share of imagination. This was what some of his workers said when he told them of his experience as he had turned into his drive and looked into the sky above his workshop.

What had caught his eye was a glittering object; golden in colour and shaped like a spinning top, stationary in the sky. Very high in the sky. The object seemed so still as to be painted in the blue sky. Adam thought that the golden colour may have been the sun reflecting on the object - for the sun was also visible high in the sky. He had put his hand to face to shield his eyes from the sun's glare and as he did, he heard Charley bark in the back. As Adam looked into the mirror to look at Charley, he noticed that Charley was focused into the sky as he had been. He quickly looked back towards the object but it had gone now - no trace, no vapour trail, no smoke or any other trace of the vision that they had both obviously observed. He searched the sky for any sign, without success.

When they arrived back at the house, Charley was in a very excited state and took some time to calm down again. Adam was also still excited and reported the matter to Jenny who calmly commented, "Really? Perhaps that pot of gold from the end of the rainbow."

Adam was not amused and responded, "possibly" and gently patted Charlie's head, Charley looked into his master's eyes as if to say, "I saw it too Pop".

The afternoon seemed to disappear in a haze as Adam considered what he had seen, his mind was simply not on the job and his workers joked about the incident. One man however did not jest and at the end of the day's work confided in Adam. Eddy had also seen something strange in the sky above the workshop - early one morning, a week earlier. The description was that the object was the same shape a humming top as Eddy described it, and Adam conceded that the description was perhaps more correct. The type of top that a child would pump from the handle on top until it reached sufficient speed to continue on it's own whilst giving out the humming sound of the gyroscopic action.   The body would stay upright until the inertia dropped off and the top would come to a halt after spinning out of control for a few moments. A fascinating toy which seemed to overcome the force of gravity and seemed magically to resist being knocked over as long as it revolved fast enough. Both men agreed that there was no sound emitted from the object they had seen. Maybe it was too high in the sky for them to hear and both commented that the object disappeared suddenly, in fact Eddy said that the object vanished as he stared at it -just like a light being switched off.

Eddy explained to Adam that this was not the first time that strange events had occurred in his life. He had experienced vivid dreams of some sort of communication with entities, beyond his means to describe, except to know instinctively that they were not human or at least not human as we understand it today. "What did he mean by this?" asked Adam. Eddy said he could not explain very well. It was a feeling of reverence, as if he were being spoken to by his priest but more so, like a young child in awe of his father and not fully understanding the communication, but he knew it was intended to be helpful. Although he was a little afraid of these strange happenings Eddy felt that there was nothing harmful and he had not spoken to anyone else of them until now.

The two of them wondered if there was any connection with the strange object that they had both seen in the same place but at different times. Neither said so but the connection was automatic and both men's minds whirled as they tried to grasp the implications. "Hmm, interesting" said Adam and resisted the temptation to make light of the situation. He could see that Eddy was not in a joking mood.

The usual reaction to such happenings, for some people, was to trivialise the event - an escape from their fear of the unknown but this was not the case with Adam. He was actually extremely serious and he would not forget what he himself had seen that day.

Chapter 3

It was a month later when Eddy failed to turn up for work. Adam was concerned because Eddy usually let him know if he was not going to be in for work, he had been absent a few times lately with nerve trouble and seemed to becoming very apprehensive and anxious about something.

Adam called Eddy's number and was answered by Doreen, Eddy's wife, who was surprised to hear that Eddy had not arrived at work as he had left as normal at 7.30 am. There was still no sign of him at 7 pm so Adam had now gone to see Doreen who was by now distraught with worry. She had phoned around all their friends and relations without success and was about to notify the police - although she knew that nothing could be done until 48 hrs had elapsed since his disappearance.

Adam agreed that she should delay in case Eddy was in some sort of trouble with the law, he also reluctantly suggested checking with the hospitals. They did both without success and when 10 o'clock arrived Adam suggested that Doreen could join him and Jenny for the night. Doreen declined the offer explaining that she wished to be home if Eddy returned. Adam said that he understood and asked her to let them know when he turned up as he was sure that he would, and she should try not to worry too much knowing that she would anyway as Eddy was not a man that did this sort of thing, ever.

That night Adam and Jenny had difficulty sleeping due to the concern for their employee and friend, however they must have dozed off in the small hours. Adam was suddenly aware that he was being spoken to by what appeared to be Eddy's voice. His first reaction was to ask him where he was.

"You wouldn't believe me if I told you" he said. "For the time being I just want you to tell Doreen that I am all right and not to worry."

"But where.... how.."

Eddy interjected again. "Please, that is all I can say at this time as I find this very difficult. I will contact you again when they are ready."

"When... who?" Adam found himself saying.

The next thing he knew he was lying in bed staring at the ceiling and wondering if he had been dreaming. He leaped out of bed with alarm when he realised what he had experienced. The time was nearly 5 am by the bedroom clock and Jenny was still sleeping - although not too soundly - and Adam got dressed quietly so as not to disturb her.

Adam was now very confused, should he tell Doreen what he had experienced? She would rightly doubt what he said, hearing Eddy's voice in a dream, dubious if anything ever was. Adam realised that to talk to Doreen about this would not be helpful and dismissed what he had heard as wishful thinking - just a dream best forgotten. Although, somehow, he felt a relief which he could not define.

Adam went down stairs and turned on the local radio station that he knew carried the 5 am news. He did not want to hear the worst but wanted to know anything that may have been reported to explain Eddy's disappearance; there was nothing, except for a number of sightings of unexplained lights in the sky around Homer. A number of people had phoned in to report these lights and one report said that the lights hovered like a helicopter but without the accompanying noise. Adam thought of his experience with the flying spinning top and wondered if there may be a connection. He had not reported anything of this due to fear of ridicule and after all he was still not convinced of what he actually saw himself.

By 7 am he "phoned Doreen to see if she had any news. What she said astonished Adam. She too it seems had had a dream, in which Eddy told her that he was all right and not to worry and that he had contacted Adam who would probably not tell her, thinking he was dreaming. The reality of the communication may be better accepted in this way. Adam verified the fact and both were astounded. Neither could fully accept the communication as fact and felt somewhat dazed by events, unable to understand what was happening. They were to find out.

Doreen was becoming frantic and was not thinking clearly. Adam however was beginning to consider a connection with the unusual sightings. For a short time he even considered that maybe Eddy had been killed and was communicating from the grave via a medium for example, he shuddered and told himself he must control this imagination of his. His mind was exploring all avenues for a solution to a situation that was getting stranger. He did not know that it was to get a whole lot stranger yet.

That day nothing further developed until nightfall when Adam was closing his workshop for the night. His staff had left an hour before and Jenny was in the house preparing the

19

evening meal. Adam and Charley were checking doors and windows when Charley suddenly started whining and cowered down into a corner of the porch to the workshop. Adam looked down at him in puzzlement and became aware of a beam of light reflected in the dog's eyes. He swung around quickly to see the source of the beam. There in the sky directly behind him was the light, nothing unusual in its appearance, a white light of moderate brilliance but stationary in the sky and totally silent.

Both were afraid of what they were seeing, Adam realising that the lack of noise was strange. He first considered it to be a balloon but could see no shape behind the light. After running around to get a better view he found that this had no effect and the light appeared the same from all angles. Jenny came running from the house as she had also seen the light from the kitchen window.

"What is it?" she called, as she neared Adam. They both stood still just gazing at the light.

After what seemed like an age but was probably only about five minutes, the light switched off and nothing was visible in the sky where it had been. Charley came, tail wagging, to greet Jenny, both people however paid little attention to the dog as they looked quizzically towards one another.

Adam broke the silence by asking if she had made a wish. "That was no shooting star", she exclaimed but don't ask me what it was."

" I think someone is trying to tell us something," said Adam.

He was more correct than he himself realised and he was about to find out what it was.

The couple discussed what they might have seen that evening with no conclusions but Adam felt that there was some connection with Eddy's disappearance. This view was reinforced when next morning Jane, Adam's daughter, said she had dreamt that Eddy was telling her to get her father to concentrate on the light. This surprised Adam as neither of them had said anything to Jane about the light, so as not to alarm her. She further informed her father that she had spoken back to Eddy asking him, "what light?" and "where was he calling from?" as though it was a phone call. "He will understand" Eddy had replied, "it is very important".

Adam was even more confused but was beginning to realise that Eddy was endeavouring to get some message through to him. Later in the day the Police arrived at the house. It seemed others had observed the light and reported it to the Police. Adam explained what had happened and assured them that he had nothing to do with the production of this light. They accepted this due to the fact that there had been many other reports of similar sightings all over the Homer district. No explanation was yet forthcoming. By now Adam was convinced that the sightings and the disappearance of Eddy were all part of what was happening to Doreen, Jane and himself. What was to happen next was to show the connection and the reason.

It was around 3 am that Adam heard Eddy's voice again. He was saying that in future he would be communicating through Jane, who was more responsive to telepathy and able to return thoughts better than Doreen or Adam. "Please take notice of what she says for this could be the most important communication since God spoke to Moses". Adam was thinking that such things might frighten Jane when Eddy interrupted his thoughts and reassured him that she was not afraid and felt it an honour to be chosen for the task. This aspect of the events had obviously been considered and resolved and Adam felt relief as well as bewilderment. But what on earth was this all about? A very good question it seems, because what Jane was to relate in the next few days was precisely what was going on here on earth.

Chapter 4

Jane was up early next morning and so was Adam. Jenny had an uneasy feeling as to just what was happening to them all and so she too was up with them making breakfast. The atmosphere was strange and Jane and Adam knew, without saying, what had happened but needed to confirm to each other that they were not just dreaming. This they did over the cereal and then when Jenny sat down to join them, with a frown on her face having over-heard the weird conversation, they told her the facts.

For Jenny, being a down to earth type of person, this was some sort of send up. However after some time of telling them "not to be silly" and that "they must have been dreaming", it registered with her that their faces were deadly serious and they were in no mood to be silly. "Oh come on you can't be serious", said Jenny and her half smile turned to a deep frown. "My god you are!"

The phone rang and Doreen spoke in a state of panic. After some calming down she was able to relate that she had heard from Eddy. Jenny told her to come over right away, then remembered that Eddy had taken the car when he disappeared, the car had also disappeared. She told her not to worry, Adam would collect her.

The workshop had to be opened and the staff attended to before Adam could do anything else. When the staff arrived there was more alarm and surprise as John, the youngest member of the team, reported a dream in which he heard Eddy and Jane talking. It was as though he were listening in to a party line he said, and felt weak in the legs when Adam said that maybe he was not dreaming and confirmed his experience.

By 9 am they were to realise that they were not the only ones to hear the communications the previous night. Radio reports were coming in about lights in the sky and as the day went on it soon became apparent that many people had experienced the same dream or "broadcast" as the media were now calling it. The connection with the light and the reference to the light it seems had prompted the calls otherwise people may have just ignored what they heard as a dream and forgotten about it. Some may have just got caught in the rush as their reports were wild exaggerations and bore no resemblance to what Jane had experienced.

Adam went to fetch Doreen and brought her back to the house. The family assembled in the living room around the fireplace where a log fire was burning, as the weather had turned quite cold. Jane was only fifteen years old but was articulate beyond her years, she attended a very good school but she would not be attending today.

If they had been sitting around the table in the dining room, this meeting could have been misconstrued as a seance. However Jane was only passing on information she had received in the early hours. She explained that Eddy had said that he was fine and well but being held by a force not recognised by him as belonging to this world. Indeed they had told him they were not, but they were here to help and not to harm anyone. "Tell Doreen I'm OK and hope to be back soon. They need me as a communicator and that's all. I feel quite important and privileged however I am not able to sleep much and they tell me they will help me to rest". He will be in contact again soon but cannot communicate for long periods. They are working on our methods of communication, which are alien to them.

As Jane finished and closed her mouth all others were wide open in disbelief, eventually Adam turned to Doreen and reassured her as a tear rolled down her already reddened cheek. "We must believe what we are told and Eddy is all right."

Jenny being more of a sceptic, thought that if this was some sort of a hoax, it was in very bad taste.

The phone rang a few times that day, people who recognised names and wanted to know more. It was apparent that the communication was not confined to Jane and others with certain perception were unwilling eavesdroppers, not all were unwilling but all were curious. They were all told that there must be some mistake - as Adam felt some privacy was desirable at this time and all in the house agreed. Doreen stayed with the Briant's for the rest of the day and on the advice of Jenny would stay the night too.

The day passed without any further developments and seemed to last an eternity for the people in the house their normal routine was forgotten and minds boggled at the possibilities of the situation and the impossibility for normality.

Night came, the light failing earlier now each night, as autumn drew on, a sharp chill was felt not only because of the dropping temperature, there was trepidation of the unknown and uncertainty, and the atmosphere was strange. Even Charley knew that tonight was different, he sat on the hearth looking sympathetically at Doreen as though he sensed her distress. He placed a paw on her lap and whined and she cuddled his head in gratitude.

The news on TV that night carried a report on the force produced by matter and anti-matter combining, the scientists had discovered that this sort of energy production was possible a score or more years after Star Trek and the propulsion unit of the Enterprise. Adam thought to himself that they aren't too far behind these day's. Science fiction has a habit of becoming science fact and he wondered at the connection. Could the ideas be implanted in the minds of the imaginative to be passed on to the more practical? He thought of Leonardo de Vinci and recognised that sometimes the abilities reside in one person. Implanted by whom from where, or was it just a flash in the pan by individuals. Ancient Greek Mythology portrayed the god Zeus's daughters as muses who inspired people to achievement. So often discoveries are made in different parts of the world at the same time, by people with no connection with one another. Because of this it is often difficult to attribute the credit for a discovery or invention. Adam was always in wonder of such things. One recent line of research which interested him greatly was the way in which plants convert sunlight into energy and a recent report had told that we now understand this process. This could have untold benefits if more efficient solar cells could be produced, and the reliance on oil based fuels could be reduced. This latter thought was closer to the present situation than Adam could have known. Plant life has existed longer than any other lifeform on earth and we are only now beginning to understand some of the secrets, a surprise was in store for the human race in the next few days.

Chapter 5

The Briant household expected to be contacted by telepathy via Jane in her sleep, but they were wrong.

It was just before 6 am when the household was awakened abruptly by a noise not unlike a tube train coming into a station. A loud rushing wind blasted the house and as they opened their eyes the occupants were aware of a flood of light through the gaps and edges of the curtains. The light was gone before anyone got to the windows.

The rushing sound continued at a lessened level and as Jane got to the window, her bedroom was the nearest to the sound, what she saw caused her eyes to widen to saucer like proportions. In the darkness she could make out the figure of a man. Behind the man was a dark shape, stopped in the air at a height of around 10 metres, stopped being a better word than hover as the object was completely still in the air, no movement at all, it just stood there like a building.

A faint conical beam outlined the figure of the man who was approaching the house and as she watched the beam disappeared, as did the dark shape. She still did not see the beam or the object move - it just turned off like a projection. The man however was still there moving towards the front door.

Adam was by this time downstairs and looking through the kitchen window which was on the front of the house. He recognised the man immediately. It was Eddy in his working clothes.

Eddy raised his hand in recognition and indicated to the door to which he was moving.

"My god, what's going on Eddy? Come inside."

The two men moved through to the living room as everyone else in the house arrived except for Charley who sat crouched in his basket in the corner of the kitchen.

Eddy embraced his wife and both were crying with relief. "Have I got a tale for you?" he exclaimed with a serious face. "But first, put the kettle on Jenny".

"What was that noise and....and thing?" said Jane still trembling from the experience.

"Later love, later" he whispered, "let's all calm down first."

Over the tea and biscuits Eddy settled down to tell the story of what had happened to him.

On the day of his "disappearance" Eddy had made his way to work as usual down the by-pass before turning off down the country road that leads to the Briant's. As he turned off, he saw the glint of sunlight reflected from a golden coloured craft that was stationary in the sky above the road. The sky and countryside seemed to change colour as though watching a TV with a colour fault. The car's steering became light and the engine stopped. He then realised that the car was airborne and events became dreamlike. As he looked at the craft he appeared stationary but when he looked down he saw he was moving at great speed, as though part of the craft above him but the height was incredible.

The fields were tiny and the town he saw as a small darker patch to the south. The shock took his breath away and his heart was pounding like a frightened rabbit. There was strangely no sense of movement apart from the visual. The unusual colours remained and he suddenly felt lethargic and slumped back into the seat.

He must have passed out or fallen asleep - whatever, he lost consciousness. The next thing he recalled was waking up wondering where he was, as you do when you sleep somewhere strange, and this he realised was somewhere extremely strange.

As he looked around the walls of the room seemed to glow with a bluish light and there was no sign of a door. He looked down to see what he was lying on and was shocked to see the floor about a metre below him and nothing else. There was no bed or mattress, he was suspended in mid-air but extremely comfortable he thought. The floor was the same as the walls and all corners were rounded and no joins or welds were evident. The ceiling was similar, with no light fittings, there were however what appeared to be vents of some sort which rotated slowly.

He slid a leg over his invisible bed and his foot dropped over the not so obvious edge. He shuffled over carefully until both legs were over and sat up. Weird he thought, and for some reason compared his situation to being in hospital and joked to himself "mental hospital perhaps". Perhaps the sanitised, strange but simplistic atmosphere? There was a faint smell of something unusual that he could not identify to himself, but this added to the hospital-like ambience.

The wall on one side started to change colour, it became paler until it became transparent and a message appeared on it like some enlarged TV screen. The message said, FEAR NOT! Like some biblical statement. Then it resumed its normal appearance.

You must be joking, he thought to himself. But somehow he did feel reassured by this message. Whoever or whatever had abducted him wished to reassure him. What next he thought? Experiments, tests, bisection, brain probes, preparation for consumption maybe, or was he attributing too many human traits to his captors?

His attention turned to the bed he was sitting on. He stood up and examined it, well, he tried too but as he could not see it he had to feel. It felt like a very soft mattress but had hardly any depth, the thickness of a piece of paper between his fingers. As he rose from the bed he also noticed that a red light came on in the wall. He moved his hand towards the light, which immediately went off. To his surprise when he went to touch the bed again it was no longer there and he walked around where he had been sitting without hindrance.

His spirits were raised somewhat by the vision he had of an alien forgetting to switch on the bed and falling to the floor.

The wall cleared again and another message read; "You have to help!"

"Who are you?" he shouted, "where am I?"

"You are onboard the I.G.V. 2M2839. We are here to warn you and all the people of your planet of your breach of natural laws

which will cause your destruction if you continue".
"What laws and what breach?"

"The natural laws are those by which all inhabited planets survive. It may be difficult to understand but we have detected signals of distress from your plant life, the plants you call trees particularly, these are the strongest transmitters of botanical communication".

"You mean the trees have informed on us?"

"You may indeed say that! We are able to monitor signals from all life forms and the transmission from your trees is a distress signal".

"Then you're here to save our trees."

"We are here to enforce the law so that you may survive your ignorance of the law".

"Why am I here? Am I some sort of hostage?"

"You have been brought here to help us to communicate, our methods are very different from your own, and we need you for what you call research".

"Research! Are you going to kill me?"

"No, rest in peace".

"You could have phrased that better!"

"We do not understand!"

"It doesn't matter. Where are you from?"

"We come from the planetary system around the twin star system you call Cirrus 2".

"How like earth is your planet?"

"Our home planet is not pronounceable in your language but it translates as "Garden", but we have also colonised many other planets and artificial worlds".

"You mean that you have created worlds?"

"We have constructed self-contained worlds - or what you may call space stations - of larger volume than your own, but enough of us; we are here because of your kind's lifestyle. The oxygen breathing species of your planet are at risk of extinction!"

"I think we are aware of the threat of pollution, the greenhouse effect and the Ozone layer problem."

"The threat to your kind is more imminent than you realise; you could be visited by a plague of such enormous proportions that would result in your exodus. We must study your brain patterns to serve our purpose. We could communicate as we are doing now, but our communications would be picked up by all and so create panic".

"You want to communicate via my brain patterns?"

"We wish to communicate with your kind as we communicate with one another, by telepathy. In this way we can achieve much more, it can impart much more than words alone".

"Can I be sure that no harm will come to me?"

"We would not attempt any research that could harm the subject, that is our way. Trust in us we have much more experience in these matters than your kind and we have safeguards to prevent damage to a subject, believe in us we beseech you".

"I have a feeling I can," said Eddy, and meant it.

"Please rest for now, you have found the bed control, we will provide food when you have rested and settled."

The messages faded and the wall resumed its original appearance.

Eddy moved his hand towards the red light and the bed appeared, this time he could see it, now it appeared as a red sheet of light across the compartment. He touched it first to test its authenticity and then sat down. The bed felt so comfortable that he swung his legs up and lay on top. His thoughts were racing and his concern turned to Doreen and what she would be thinking as his consciousness of this strange environment faded and he was asleep.

Chapter 6

Eddy awakened to find that he was in a different room, much larger than the compartment that he occupied previously. He sensed the presence of someone standing behind his head and there was a movement but before he could turn to look he felt his head being held or restricted by some kind of headgear, at this point he felt the flow of adrenaline that comes with fear.

He tried to speak but found that he could not make a sound. Then he heard a voice say, "have no fear" he recognised the phrase and immediately felt some relief, as the voice seemed to impart more than the words said.

"I am communing with you by telepathy" said the voice, "raise your hand if you understand".

He raised his right hand and when he realised he could move, tried to sit up. He could not, he was held by some unseen restraint.

"Is it necessary to tie me down?" he said.

"For your own protection it is desirable, be calm." And he was.

The room was lined with coloured lights of many different colours and shapes. They were however only in the top half, the height he estimated to be around 3 metres. He recognised that they appeared to be within the wall and not mounted on the wall, like the bed switch.

"You are correct in your observations", the voice said. "They are switches and controls and they may be operated by thought intention as long as the intention is lawful and from the correct source. We are enhancing your powers to communicate by telepathy so that you may pass on the things that we wish to impart and reassure your own. It is also necessary to enable us to commune with your kind on a larger scale."

"Do you intend to release me?"

"Yes soon, have no fear."

"Easy to say for you, not so easy me to accept"

"You seem to be responding well.... Eddy."

"How do you know my, err, oh... I get it. It doesn't appear to work in the other direction, I don't read any thoughts from you other than your intended message."

"No that is not yet intended, forgive our intrusion, it is of necessity that we do this."

"Why do you use the word commune as well as communicate?"

"Because we intend to achieve both, it is desirable to the benefit of many kinds that we do."
"Can I look at you?"

The figure behind his head moved around the side of the bed that Eddy lay on. Eddy's nerves began to twitch as the figure came into his view, his eyes widened in surprise. He did not know what to expect but what his eyes focused on he did not expect. He was looking at his friend and employer... ADAM!

"What the.... Adam is it you?"

"Not yet," was the reply, "we are able to clone anyone or anything and we will have to use this ability to achieve are aims".

 "What are your aims," said Eddy.

"We have told you, to help you and others of your planet to survive."

"So you did - but why and how?"

"One step at a time friend, the time and place is important, we must not cause panic or misinterpretation of our purpose."

The new Adam went on to explain that Eddy would be able to communicate with Doreen after his treatment but this would be easier to begin with whilst she was asleep. In fact as already described, communication was first made with Adam and then Jane, the latter being found to be the more receptive and as his ability improved he was able to get through to Doreen, Jane it was found, could also return the contact most effectively.

The fact that others had picked up the transmissions, (although they, the recipients, were not sure if they were dreaming or not), was not expected and their plans had to be changed for the time being. It seems that their studies of Earth's history had focused on the real panic caused by the science fiction radio play, "The War of the Worlds." This told them a lot about human nature and behaviour and they were particularly sensitive to human response, which resulted in this shyness and indirect contact.

"Safer all around if they played it low profile," said Eddy "and that's why I am back here to tell the tale directly. A cautionary tale if ever there was one - I can tell you."

His audience was open-mouthed still and when they had absorbed the enormity of what they found themselves involved in, were dumbfounded, until Adam broke the silence.

"What are they here for Eddy?"

"The trees" said Eddy, "they have been talking to the trees.

 You could say the trees have split on us.

They are capable of interpreting signals given out by vegetation. They have knowledge of life forms that we are not yet capable of understanding, we have only just discovered how to replicate how a plant converts the sun's energy and celebrate this as a great step forward. They have discovered how plants communicate and in a way they can understand and talk back.

Many of us talk to our treasured plants and claim that they grow the better for it. The others say we are mad. Man has talked to the trees for centuries - maybe they were listening all the time?   But let's not take this lightly, the signals from our plants, the trees in particular as the largest best designed transmitter, have started to give out distress signals that warn others of their kind of the dangers of human pillage and pollution.

The trees are the lungs of the Earth creating oxygen and

absorbing carbon dioxide. Without them we would not have been able to live, or continue to live. "We can live for days without food or water but only minutes without oxygen and yet we take it for granted that it will always be there. Past generations respected the trees for the part they played in human life without realising that they provided the very air that we breathe. They provided refuge from animals, shade from the sun, shelter from the rain, distant views of the prey or enemies, food in the form of fruits, housing, furniture, ships, rubber, cork, and fuel to name a few examples."

Jane interrupted "but Uncle Eddy what are *they* here for, to stop us chopping the trees down?"

"Err.. yes, it must be stopped," said Eddy, looking at Adam sympathetically.

Adam sensed that there was something that Eddy was reluctant to speak about, he also twigged that it was Jane's presence that inhibited him. Unfortunately Jane being a perceptive child also caught the reluctance and pursued the questioning.

"Do they intend us any harm?" she said.

"No!" said Eddy with assurance, "that is not their purpose, they are here to help."

"Us or the trees?" said Jenny in her practical straight to the point way.

"Both" said Eddy, "the planet as a whole really, you might say."

Jenny "mmmd" distrust and collected the cups.

Doreen was stunned into silence and Adam's eyes sparkled with interest and awe.

"At last!" said Adam with the air of Livingstone meeting Stanley, but he was still concerned about the "Err..", which had preceded Eddy's reply to young Jane. He wanted to talk to Eddy alone for this reason but with such a perceptive family floundered for a way without causing alarm.

Eddy was obviously tired and Doreen quietly intervened and suggested that he should get some rest.

"Please stay here till daylight, you're in no state to travel" said Jenny as she returned still clutching the tea towel in her hands. "I'll get you some breakfast and then see how you feel."

Jane pulled back the curtains and looked intensely into the night sky.

"Come away said Jenny", nervously, her down to earth practicality wearing thin and a sense of fear of the unknown overtaking her.

"Mum I can sense something strange," said Jane. "I can feel, (she paused for thought to find the right words) well... like... Christmas Eve."

"Well that's not so far away," said Jenny, "I think you should go back to bed. Come on let's go, I'll come with you," and they both went upstairs.

Doreen went to the bathroom looking keenly at her husband with some disbelief in her eyes as she closed the door behind her.

Adam seized the opportunity to question Eddy more fully, whilst, at the same time, Eddy started to explain so that both had to stop and start again. Eddy gestured to Adam to calm down and went on to spell out that there was more to the story than he had yet told. "We are in danger," he said.

"From these Visitors" said Adam.

"No," said Eddy, "not according to them anyway. As I said before they are here to help against the danger."

"Then what?" said Adam impatiently.

"The Trees themselves" said Eddy, "they have the ability to ward off parasites by their secretions and even poison them."

"Yes I know that," said Adam.

"Well," replied Eddy they have identified humans as parasites."

"You mean that the timber will become poisonous to touch?"

"I'm afraid the threat is much more than that" said Eddy looking down at his hands reluctant to pass on the ultimatum.

"Unless we take positive action to preserve sufficient woodland area the fruits will become poisonous to man. The air we breath will not only become deficient in oxygen but instead of them giving out oxygen, they will start to exude oxides of poisons of all kinds, depending on the type of plant, but all will be deadly to human beings. The threat is all too real when you think of the poisons produced by plant life such as toadstools, deadly nightshade, foxgloves, not to mention the more exotic equatorial varieties of plants. If the largest, strongest, most common, oldest grandfather of all living things turned nasty it wouldn't need to walk, but we would need to run, and we would find it difficult to find sanctuary on this world."

Adam screwed up his eyes in disbelief. Man-killing trees took some believing. The most helpful plant to man has no need of man and should he become a threat, goodbye man. Makes sense in a human perspective if they had a human perspective maybe we would have been dead years ago.

Adam's thoughts turned to the Visitors with the message, "These messengers," he said, "where are they from and what is their angle?"

"Later" said Eddy, who by now was closing his eyes involuntarily with physical and emotional exhaustion.

"Lie down on the couch Eddy and get some sleep," said Jenny as she returned to the room. He was soon asleep and the three still awake, looked at each other in bewilderment. Well they would wouldn't they?

Chapter 7

Daylight broke on a bright but cold morning. The sky was clear when Jane, the first to rise, looked out into the clear blue sky and wondered if she had dreamed the happenings of the last few days.

Two ominous black clouds to the north caught her eye. As she watched, they grew larger and spread over towards the east and the sun which was just rising above the trees of the copse on Johnson's hill which rose to the east of the Briant's property. The trees were mainly tall straight pines which towered like giants frozen in time, at this time in the morning the sun seemed to rest on them for a while as though bracing itself for its day's journey across the heavens.

Jane looked over to the clouds and the Christmas Eve feeling of the night before seemed marred with a kind of foreboding which caused her to shiver with a sudden chill. "Something is about to happen" she whispered to herself. Her senses seemed to tell her that this was just a beginning. Before the sun went to roost in the Oaks of the western horizon she would know she was right.

Over breakfast the atmosphere was tense and the discussion guarded from the male members of the household. As it was Saturday, Adam would not be opening the workshop. He asked Eddy what the Visitor's views of his business would be.

"I would say their concern was more with the destruction of trees to make way for concrete and tarmac than what we do," said Eddy. "Not to forget the wholesale demolishing of rain-forests for profits and land reclamation. Botanists have protested for years now about these things, governments too."

"Hypocritically since the same governments have ignored envi-ronmental considerations for centuries before" added Adam. "Perhaps ignorance is an excuse when it comes to natural law, at least we hope so."

"For they know not what they do," whispered Jane. "Forgiveness becomes more difficult when the offender is aware of the crime."

Eddy reassured them all that it was not to punish or judge that the Visitors were here but to warn!

"Lets pray they are truthful these.... Visitors," said Doreen.

"Yes they are" blurted out Jane, blushing with embarrassment at her own conviction. She felt instinctively that these were good, not evil beings.

"I'm sure you're right love" said Eddy "really I am." His eyes turned to Adam and then to Jenny with a reassuring smile on his face, then back to his bacon and egg.

Adam was too tense to eat breakfast and settled for dunking a digestive in his coffee.

"I think there's a storm brewing Dad", said Jane.

"You could be right Janey better batten the hatches," Adam replied and he went into the yard to check on the workshop.

As he passed by the window in the door to the workshop he saw a movement inside and decided to open up and check. He walked slowly between the machines. Charley would usually be behind him at this point but today was different, he had stayed behind in the house. Adam thought it strange but put it down to the fact that Charley liked people and wanted to stay with the guests in the house. He was soon to find out that he was wrong.

Charley may have sensed something, or been influenced by something. Between the bandsaw and the planing machine Adam Briant came face to face with Adam Briant.

Both stood fixed on one another, the real Adam frowning and the other smiling. The other intoning - what would seem to be their kind's common greeting - "Fear not, I come to help you."

Unfortunately, Eddy had not got around to telling Adam of the talents of impersonation that the Visitors possessed. As a result of his ignorance, Adam thought the man to be an ordinary intruder and proceeded to round on him, verbally that is, as he was not a violent man. The opening line of the Visitor was somewhat unusual to say the least, that apart, anyone would be reticent to clobber someone who looks like one's own mirror image.

"What are you doing here, who are you, how did you get in?"

"Patience friend" said the impostor. "Forgive me if I shocked you, but verily we must talk with you."

44

"Then talk boyo and make it snappy!" said Adam trying to sound tough and unafraid. "Fear not?" "Verily?" he thought. Peculiar, maybe some cult weirdo or religious nut. Although he had a strong faith he did not hold with extremists of any kind.

"You should not think of your kind in such derisory terms," said the Visitor.

"What do you mean my kind," said Adam, "and for that matter how did you know what I was thinking." The light was beginning to dawn in his head and he realised that this was not a man from this world.

"You're a Visitor aren't you, you're the ones who kidnapped Eddy".

"I am one of the Visitors who are here to help you." he replied.

"Help?" said Adam. "All that you've done so far is frighten us to death."

"I perceive that no one has died as a result of our presence, why do you say this?"

"It's just a figure of speech" Adam responded sheepishly, as though he had been caught out in some deliberate lie.

"Our aim is to prevent death on a scale you could not imagine."

"So I am led to believe said Adam" with more than a slight hint of disbelief in his tone."

"You would do well to heed our warning Adam. You must help yourselves and do as we suggest or you and your kind may not survive the storm. Remember Noah? Circumstances may require another but very different type of Ark this time."

"How can we alter anything, why have you come here."

"You and this sector have been chosen as the most responsive according to our sensors. You have been chosen as our spokesman to the rest of your kind."

"Suppose I don't wish to be."

"You will, we know it, you and your family, along with others will be transported if the need arises."

"Transported to where?" said Adam.

The Visitor made a gesture to him to stop talking, raising a hand with the palm towards him and said that his time had elapsed and he must return. A beam of light pierced down through the roof before the Visitor's hand was lowered to his side, the light engulfed the Visitor and he faded out. The light disappearing as quickly has it had come.

The only trace remaining of the Visitor was a faint smell that Adam now recognised had been there from the time he opened the door. The smell was similar to a freshly struck match. Faint but recognisable amongst the smell of wood and varnish. He checked around to make sure there was no fire or other damage, there was none.

Back in the house no one was aware of this most recent incident and Doreen and Eddy prepared to go back home. Adam returned to the house with mixed feelings of what had happened. This was something that he had always wanted but the reason for the visit was due to imminent peril and that took away all feeling of celebration. This threat, he was in no doubt, was to the human race as a whole and to oxygen breathing life in it's entirety - the end of the world.

When he got back to the house he was noticeably shaken and pale. Jenny asked him if he was all right and led him to a chair. He told his story and Eddy apologised for not telling him about the cloning. "There was so much to remember and it was such a shock to the system and maybe I just didn't want to tell you yet."

"Don't worry about it Eddy, there is so much more to..", he was going to say worry about but diplomatically changed it to "consider."

Jane shouted from the kitchen "look there over the workshop." Jenny went over to join her and saw what Jane saw but by the time the others got there it was gone. "My god" said Jenny "I saw it." Jane was in a daze.

"What's the matter Jane," her mother said, sensing that she was in some sort of a trance.

Flipping back to reality she burst out, "they spoke to me," she said, "they said that they would need me later but to have no fear."

The figure of speech was familiar to Eddy and Adam and they knew they had indeed communicated with Jane. She found it amusing and exciting and was not afraid in slightest. "It was the golden globe that you saw," said Jenny. "It was above the workshop just clear of the roof, it was about 10m. in diameter and I could see someone inside through the windows."

Jenny's cool practicality had deserted her and she was clearly afraid of what she had seen and in particular its interest in her daughter. She had doubted the stories she had heard from her friends and family and could not accept them as fact, until know!

"Adam it was you, I saw you in that thing."

Adam and Doreen tried to calm Jenny, whilst Eddy rushed to the door in vain – the shape had gone. Never-the-less he shouted into the sky and if they did hear him they would need an Anglo-Saxon interpreter to understand! It appeared that he did not approve of the way they were going about things and suggested a suitable location for a piece of unplaned 3x2 he had picked up and was waving at the sky.

Eddy and Doreen's plans to go home would be shelved if these incidents were to continue. Strength in numbers would seem to be the rule of the day. Reports to the police were considered but before they could be made, events overtook them as the police arrived in force, three carloads to be precise. One patrol car, an unmarked car and a personnel carrier (riot control type) brakes screeching movie style as they pulled up to the house.

The occupants of the personnel carrier surrounded the workshop and shouted loudly to one another.

"What the hell's going on" said Adam.

The inspector, climbing out of the unmarked car with some difficulty as it was still moving. "Where are they? We have had reported sitings of a flying object over your property" he said breathlessly.

"You're too late mate" said Eddy "but stick around they will be back!"

"Who are you sir?" said the inspector.

"Eddy Barton from Fulton, who are you?"

"Chief Inspector Critchwell, Homer Police Dept."

Adam, still taken back by events, came forward to introduce himself. He explained that Eddy was the reported missing man and that they had a tale to tell and invited the inspector inside. The inspector beckoned to a subordinate to accompany him and they went inside, leaving the rest of the party poking around for evidence. They would not find any!

Inside, the policeman explained that reports of abductions had prompted his response and Adam confirmed that Eddy had in fact been abducted but the abductors appeared to mean no harm.

"Allow me to determine that sir," he said. "Abduction is a crime regardless of intent. Now Mr. Barton please, I presume you will be bringing charges, can you give me a description of the offenders."

"Yes" said Eddy "sitting next to you. I think this may take some time."

Adam smiled slightly. "You say abductions in the plural, have there been others."

"Quite a few said the policeman Mr.Barton was one of twenty reported on the same day, and others have been returned like him. There are some reports from their relatives, that they would appear to have had personality changes. What about Mr. Barton?"

"No, still the obstinate Eddy said Adam."

"I think you'll find that they could be clones," said Eddy, "I'd better tell you the whole story although you'll probably lock me up anyway - in a padded cell I shouldn't wonder."

As Eddy and Adam were about to tell their story, the policeman's phone started to ring. "Excuse me" he said politely "one of the drawbacks of modern technology."

He suddenly sat upright in recognition of a superior, "yes sir rightaway sir" he said after two or three minutes of intense listening.

"That was head office," he said. "we've been called off. "What the heck is going on, we have been called off" he said. "Thank you gentlemen, come on Bates get'em together we're out of here!"

Just then a jet fighter whistled over the house as Critchwell, on cue, said, "The Air Force has taken over, we are on a defensive alert, the balloon would appear to have gone up."

The police departed as quickly as they had arrived, wheels spinning and dust flying. When everyone in the house had got their breath back, they again looked to the sky as the noise of helicopters pervaded the atmosphere. Three helicopters in "V" formation passed over the house and then spread out in a search pattern, a fourth of a different insignia approached and landed close to the house.

"What is happening," said Jenny, now getting annoyed with events." Tears started to flow and some consoling was necessary from Jane who seemed to be coping as well as anyone.

Adam went out to meet the occupants of the helicopter who turned out to be an Air Force officer named Caplow and an airman, who was not introduced, his calling card being an automatic handy and ready for action.

"I hope that is not necessary" said Adam gesturing to the gun.

"So do I" said the officer, "just insurance. Now what can you tell us about these flying machines."

"The message they bring is more important," said Adam.

"Did you see any weapons?" said the officer."

"No but...."

"How large would you estimate it to be?" Caplow interrupted.

"They mean us no harm" said Adam.

"Which direction did they go."

"None," said Adam feeling himself getting annoyed by Caplow's attitude.

"I warn you that to withhold information will result in your arrest, we are in a defensive alert situation here."

"I repeat sir, they took no direction, they just disappeared! 0° East 0° West 0° North 0° South, please follow them!" said Adam now quite annoyed.

The pilot shouted that there had been a sighting and both men raced back to the 'copter.

"God help us," Adam muttered!

Back in the house events continued to accelerate, Jane had gone into another trance and was talking in a strange style that was not her own. "We need to take you on board" she said, please trust us and do as we say." She was obviously being used by the Visitors as they had indicated that they would.

Adam asked if this was necessary, as the inference was that they might need to take the whole family on board if things went wrong.

"Things are not going to plan!" Jane replied after a pause that suggested that the Visitors were being very careful with their answers. "However with your help, particularly your daughter we may be able to convince your leaders of our purpose. We would assume that you would wish to accompany your daughter and others amongst you that may be of use to the cause."

It was difficult to listen to Jane speaking about herself, but they did recognise that the Visitors were using her as a two-way radio. She continued. "Please collect a small amount of necessary luggage for your customary hygiene. We must leave within 15 min. You must gather together within a circle of 1 metre diameter."

"Do we need to be outside" said Adam.

"No" came the reply, "stay inside the house but please be as quick as possible, time is running out."

Jane turned to her mother and said "it's all right Mum, they are good people. Trust them

"They may never return us" said Jenny "how can we trust them?"

"I think you can," said Eddy, "after all they returned me didn't they?".

Adam was deep in thought; "they may be our only hope" he eventually came out with.

"If you can believe what they say," retorted Jenny, "and I don't know if I do."

"There comes a time in every life when a major decision must be made, and they don't come any bigger than this do they?"

"They need our daughter to help save mankind?" Questioned Jenny, "can that be real?"

"They don't really need to intervene at all do they? The least we can do is co-operate," said Adam, "I think we should."

"So do I," said Eddy, "we must try, I have a feeling we were intended to do this, it feels right to me and I think they need some human assistance if they are to succeed. They are strangers here after all, and don't know all they should, that's obvious. What do you say Doreen?"

"I'm staying with you this time whatever," she said, with a very serious look. "Looks like I'm outnumbered doesn't it. Help me get the things together Janey, and may the Lord protect us all."

The decision was made and they were about to start on a journey, which would be somewhat further and a lot stranger than any of them could have anticipated.

Chapter 8

The party of six, not forgetting Charley, as they had no intentions of leaving him behind, was ready for departure after ten minutes of hectic preparation. They stood and held each other's hands like New Year's Eve with Charley in the middle looking up at Adam questioningly.

There was a whiff of a newly struck match and a sudden flood of light and they all drew closer together. Some of them had their eyes closed; Adam looked around to see what was happening. They were standing on the living room carpet, which faded as Adam looked down as he felt the floor beneath his feet seem to fall away like a lift starting to descend. That was the only feeling of movement that was felt and within seconds they were standing huddled together in a room the size of which was similar to the living room they had just left but dissimilar in all other ways.

The room was light but no artificial lights were evident neither were there any windows. A voice spoke quietly and warmly from a direction which was uncertain saying, "welcome aboard to you all, have no fear, we are attempting to help you and your kind. Please make yourselves comfortable, there are rests around the walls with which Eddy is familiar.

Thank you for returning Eddy, we are grateful."

"I hope you are worthy of these good people's trust," said Eddy.

"We have put ourselves in your hands" Adam added.

"We appreciate your trust and we will meet you personally, but first you must be prepared."

The party followed Eddy to the walls of the room where he found the red lights, which operated the rests as the Visitors called them. The red beams lit up and Eddy gestured to the ladies to sit on the beams of light, they declined however until he demonstrated by sitting down himself, the rest then tentatively followed suit.

"H'm, quite comfortable," remarked Adam.

The eyes of the party searched around for information of their whereabouts. Charley, who was very wary and nervous, lay down by Jane's feet, with a muted growl and stared at one point on the wall.

"Reminds me of the Dentist's waiting room!" said Doreen.

Eddy recalled the hospital ambience of his previous experience and agreed. They joked nervously that the doctor's name was not displayed under the red light in the wall.

"Doctor Who?" Jane added, but no one laughed out loud.

There was now a hush of expectancy as Charley stood up and set the point on the wall that he had not taken his eyes off for the last ten minutes.

The wall opposite them lightened and Eddy expected written words to appear. However the face of a Visitor smiled back at them. All eyes immediately turned to Adam and back and back again to the screen, rather like some bizarre tennis match. They were amazed by what they saw, for again it was Adam's image.

"Fear not" said the face in the wall, "this is what we meant by prepared, some of you are already aware of the fact that we have adopted Adam's image for our purpose."

"Why not appear as you really are" said Adam.

"We feel that this is a more appropriate guise for the purpose, more comfortable for your perception perhaps. We are a crew of twelve and each of us will appear as I do."

"Twelve Adams" said Jenny.

"Thirteen with the original" replied the Visitor. "We have twelve cruiser ships each with twelve crew members all of whom have taken the likeness of their chosen spokesman. I would like to come in to you with another of our kind, so that we may provide you with the food that you require. He too will appear as Adam but each of us has a different colour-coded suit for identification and rank. I am Gold and my colleague is Silver."

"Must brighten things up when you get together" said Eddy. There was no reply and the picture faded.

"Talk about colour discrimination" said Jane in a whisper. There was a slight swishing noise and a doorway appeared in the wall to their left. Through the door, two figures entered, as expected, both identical to Adam, one dressed in gold and the

56

other in silver but each was a subtle shade such that only deliberate attention could distinguish the difference.

"They also aid recognition by our sensors" said Gold, reading the thoughts which most of those present were emitting. "We would like you to change into similar suits later, they also provide certain protection which would be advisable for you too. You will not need the colour variation as you are identifiable without."

Maybe the attention to the clothing was due to the fact that only one person in the party saw anything that they were not accustomed to seeing - and that was Adam himself, although Charley had now adopted the tennis mode confused by three masters. Eventually sniffing at each in turn and then deciding there was only one genuine. The other two, he had determined, were impostors and he eyed them with suspicion and an icy glare shared between the two.

The two Visitors had what looked like glass jars in their arms and handed one to each person. "Eat what you like when you like," said Gold "keep it in the container and it will remain fresh permanently. It is a vegetable concentrate containing all the vitamin requirements of your bodies. Water is available from the blue sensor, just think water."

No one was hungry in the slightest but they thanked their hosts. 'Where are you taking us?', was the question on the minds of most now, and in response the Visitors explained that they were not going anywhere at the moment - they were stationary.

"I thought I could not feel any movement" said Adam.

"At this moment in time" said Gold "we are 10 miles above

Vatican City." Quite a number of lower jaws dropped on chests at this point.

"You mean we are in Italy already" Adam stammered.

"We arrived as you sat down" Gold reported proudly. Just then Adam remembered the Air Force and asked if the Visitors had not encountered the jets or helicopters.

"Well we saw them but they did not see us" was the reply in a matter of fact style. "They can become very dangerous to one another you know dashing about like that." Adam detected a note of sarcasm in the Visitor's response confirmed by the latter part of the response "they are so inefficient at stopping aren't they?"

With a certain amount of relief, Adam asked why they were in Italy, if you consider 10 miles up as Italy.

"Our purpose is to talk with the most powerful man on earth".

"The Pope!" exclaimed Adam.

"I believe that is his title" said Gold, "we seek his assistance, his influence on humans would seem to be great. Also this man communicates telepathically better than any other leader"

"I think you mean prayer" Adam suggested.

"Communication with God by thought is the highest form of telepathy but perhaps not the most difficult" responded Gold.

Adam perceptively picked up on the point that Gold referred to God rather than *his* God or *your* God.

"God is God!" said Gold. "We have work to do" and both Visitors left with the door swishing into oblivion behind them; there was not the slightest trace where the door had been.

"What about that Eddy?" said Adam.

"Seem genuine, but somewhat confused I would say" said Eddy.

"Aliens that believe in God" said Adam, "that's a turn up, eh?"

Adam was a firm believer himself although he knew Eddy was a sceptic if not quite an atheist. In fact Adam was a Catholic by birth, not a devout Catholic by any means although his belief had grown with the years, and his experience confirmed his faith. To his mind however religious groups were sometimes detrimental to the truth, especially when they conflicted with one another. The only religious army without hypocrisy to his mind was the Salvation Army, which he held in great respect.

Jane was thinking water, and a blue light appeared in the wall. Eddy explained that she should move her hand towards the light but before she was anywhere near to it, a depression appeared in the wall where a fountain of water arced into a basin. She took a drink, smiled with approval, and took another. She dried her mouth on the back of her hand and the fountain disappeared without trace.

"You have powerful thoughts," said Eddy.

Her face lit up with pride "Don't I just!" she said. Thinking she might like a large box of chocolates, but to her disappointment nothing happened. She looked towards her mother and Doreen who had been very quiet so far and Jane recognised their apprehension. "You know Mum, that just reminded me of the time Grandad first tried our TV remote control, he was delighted with the effect on the TV but disappointed when it didn't work on gran." Both women laughed and the tension seemed to lessen just a little.

"You know it helps to know that these Visitors, whoever they are, believe in God," said Adam.

"Lets hope it's the same one" said Doreen.

Eddy was wearing a worried frown and did not share the amusement, "You know Adam" he said, "I think they are barking up the wrong tree, no pun intended."

"An unfortunate phrase that Eddy, but what do you mean?"

"Well perhaps the President of the United States would be more appropriate or the United Nations. I don't see how the Pope is going to bring about the changes required."

"I have a feeling that we are about to find out soon" said Adam. "I think the chance of making great changes in a little time is a bit King Canute anyway, but they are trying, why should they, what's in it for them if what they say is true?"

"I think we may soon be finding out" said Jenny, and she was right.

Chapter 9

"Mum I need to go to the bathroom" said Jane.

"I hope they've got one" replied her mother. Fortunately as she spoke there was a swish and another door opened and again her thoughts were enough to activate the required utility.

"Neat" said Jane and had no hesitation in entering the room, which had opened before her. Her mother followed to be on the safe side. The toilets were more along the lines of a French system than any other, with illuminated feet positions. Without going into too much unnecessary detail, water jets and hot air blowers provided the necessary. However on completion the whole system simply disappeared presumably until someone else had the same thought. On exiting, the door did the same disappearing trick, as expected.

"Dad this is one neat ship" said Jane to her father. "Helpful that we went to France for that holiday though."

Another swish and Gold returned. "I hope you are comfortable and getting used to your surroundings," he said. "I would like to talk with you in our debating room, we have a few problems you may be able to help us with."

The party followed in line as Gold beckoned them to follow. They passed through a corridor and into a room which to their surprise contained around thirty other people who were dressed in normal everyday clothes, all were clearly startled by each other's presence and began to ask questions of each other. "Where are you from?" "When did you get here?" etc.

They soon found that they were all from Homer County and had been brought onboard in a similar way. There was a large table, oval in shape in the centre of the room, no apparent means of support could be seen above or below. On the table were suits similar to those worn by the Visitors but all were white. Gold spoke into his hand and his voice was magnified to reach all in the room. "Please for your own protection put on the suits you see before you. Put them over your existing clothing except for heavy outerclothing."

There was frantic pulling and grunting as they did as asked. The noise level began to rise again as people fitted and talked. The material was extremely light and stretched to fit all sizes except that the children's which were obviously smaller to begin with. No zips or buttons were evident, but where the material was overlapped it stuck inside to outside not unlike Velcro but with no obvious special material.

"Are they going to give us a motorbike now" one little boy said. There were five children and a baby amongst the guests and for the baby a special tiny replica of the full size thing was provided. Adam wondered if they had been expecting just such requirements or were they manufactured there and then.

Gold commented that he hoped they were comfortable and that they would be able to move around more freely with them on. "Be seated around the table when you are ready" he added.

Gold continued "At this moment in time eleven other ships such as this are spaced around the planet Earth each one is ten miles above a major target." At which point muttering broke out, the mention of 'targets' conjured up weaponry targets. "Please! Have no fear; the targets of which I speak are *communication* targets! Forgive me I should have known that word to a civilisation such as yours, who still suffer wars, would jump to conclusions. We cannot remember war. We are peace-abiding people who mean you no harm.

"He keeps saying that," said Eddy. "And we mean it," said Gold, to Eddy's surprise, not knowing whether Gold had heard him, or would have said that anyway. He decided to keep quiet just in case. No point in upsetting them he thought.

"The major leaders of the world will be contacted by telepathy and told of the threat to your planet."

"Are we hostages said one of the guests."

"No, " said Gold "you all came here of your own freewill, except perhaps for the baby, but I feel sure Mum would have not wanted to leave her behind."

Adam sensed that Gold was now communicating in more colloquial terms than when they first met, all that verily, beseech and so forth would seem to have been from a previous era which had now been adjusted.

As if in response to Adams thoughts, Gold continued, "we have been here before but many centuries ago and this problem that you have now is even more serious than then. Our target is your Pope and our aim is to communicate the importance of preventing further attacks on the trees and other vegetation of your planet, our sensors show that you are seriously close to triggering the self preservation defences of these living organisms.

We have been aware of these defences from previous experience and would not see such things repeated if they can be avoided. The oxygen breathing creatures of your world have been destroyed before by this method and many centuries are needed to recuperate from such destruction. The dinosaurs of your past we saw destroyed in hours and the atmosphere of your planet was unbreathable by mammals for a thousand years, only small mammals survived deep in the Earth's caves. Your scientists believe it may have been a comet hitting the earth. They are incorrect, we saw it happen and it was not the first time. We are not infallible and our thesis on the trigger mechanism may be incorrect. We hope it is a trigger by way of response to destruction. Some of our scientists favour another theory but we all hope they are wrong."

"What theory is that?" asked one of the guests.

"The theory that the defence mechanism is cyclic in nature and operates on a time basis in order not to allow any mammal the time to become a threat to their continued existence."

The guests were petrified by the implication of the information they had just received. It took several minutes for the full import to sink in and before anyone broke the silence.

Adam was the first to speak. "If I understand you correctly, the options are: (a) if the theory that the trigger is threat of destruction, we have a chance of preventing it. But (b), if the theory is that every so many thousands of years or so they go off like a firework with an extra long fuse - then goodnight Vienna; London; Washington and all points west for that matter."

"I believe you have the gist Adam. Our view is swinging to

option (b) although it is possible too that both may be correct, I regret to say and history is about to repeat itself. This is why we are here with you. We too are oxygen breathers with close links and interest in your kind, we could not sit back and watch without trying to help."

"What point is there then in trying to persuade the world to stop chopping down trees." Eddy commented.

"If triggering is due to human inflicted damage alone, then if it stops, the trigger may not be activated or maybe delayed. If it is only delayed it would be an advantage, time is of the essence."

Eddy bowed his head in acceptance of the pure logic, but still pursued the argument, as was his way. "This time that we may win would seem merely to put off the inevitable."

Gold seemed a little eager at this point. "If it should come to the inevitable then you will all be needed to assist."

Another guest interjected at this point "How can we help?" said a young woman who Jane immediately recognised as one of the teachers from her school.

"Mrs Jones!" she whispered to her mother, Jenny nodded acknowledgement with a "shhh."

"We would want you to act as guides and assist in the evacuation." responded Gold. "We regret to inform you it may be the only way to save your people's seed."

"You can't rescue the whole human race, can you?" asked Adam.

"I'm afraid not Adam. But we can save some."

"How do you decide whom to save and whom to condemn to death" said Adam allowing his frustration to show.

"As it is written" said Gold, and before any further questions could be asked, requested all to return to the rooms from which they came. Great commotion followed as doors swished all around the room and people with much more uniformity, due to their suits, left the large room. The table faded and disappeared before their eyes.

"Great space savers these coloureds" remarked Jane, immediately blushing as she realised the political incorrectness of her remark, which she had no intention of inferring.

"Think before you speak Jane" said Jenny. "Ignorance is no excuse if you offend someone because of lack of forethought."

"We whites need to be saved" said Eddy trying to relieve the situation.

"I think we have more to worry about than offending anyone" said Adam grimly. "Do you realise this may be the end of the world for us."

They returned to their room where the atmosphere between them was tense as they reflected on the information that they had been given.

"Am I dreaming" said Doreen. "I can't believe all this. It's too fantastic to be real I don't think I can take much more" and she broke down in tears.

Eddy tried to comfort her. "We are safe with these people Doreen."

"We don't even know that they are people" said Doreen. "Or that they are telling us the truth."

The screen in the wall cleared and Gold appeared once more. "Thank you for listening to me, I will let you know of any developments, make yourselves comfortable and try to get some rest, we could get quite busy soon." The screen re-merged with the wall and the party sat down to await developments.

Jane thought about a mirror as she wanted to see what she looked like in here one piece white suit, within seconds a section of wall became reflective.

Charley now became restless. "I think he wants to go for a walk" said Jenny.

"A space walk?" said Adam.

Jane, by now, was getting into the environment and adapting to the way things work - as teenagers do so well. "When in Rome, Dad she said, "oh or even 10 miles above," as she only then realised where she was.

"What do you mean" said Adam."

"Well think about it, I mean literally think about it. They seem to have developed virtual reality into actual reality by the power of thought." I told you she was a perceptive girl!

"You mean think about taking Charley for a walk?"

"Well it didn't work for chocolates" she said "but it may if it's necessary."

Eddy remembered what he was told on his first visit, "if the thoughts are from the right source and legitimate." "Try it!" Eddy blurted out.

Adam was already doing so and as the rest looked on Adam and Charley faded like ghosts and finally disappeared."

"My goodness" exclaimed Jenny, "where are they?" "I think Dad's taken Charley for a walk Mum don't worry."

Adam could not believe his eyes, he was walking in the lane from their home and Charley was just as surprised to find himself there. Adam immediately made tracks for home pausing by compulsion to allow Charley to do the necessary; he felt obliged to pull Charley away from the trees and eyed them with suspicion. The thought passed through his mind that he had just emerged from a spell of amnesia and if he could get home he would find that every thing would be normal. Charley started running towards home maybe thinking similar thoughts. As Adam opened the garden gate the scene suddenly changed and they found themselves back onboard the strange craft, Adam felt as though he had awakened from a nightmare to find that the nightmare was true.

"What happened," said Jenny "where have you been?"

"I was at home" he said "at least I think I was."

Gold again appeared on screen to explain that what he had experienced was the power of the mind enhanced by their technology and that it was not in fact reality. Adam had never left the ship but was transported to an area of the ship for such purposes. Not that he meant for exercising dogs particularly but where circumstances required simulation. "Very useful on long voyages" he commented.

Well what did you expect, on an alien spaceship, a poop scoop!

Chapter 10

Time passed quickly with such developments and most people had lost track of what time of day it was but their body clocks were now indicating that it was time to sleep. Eddy was already snoring loudly as he was the one of the party who felt some relief. Considering his experience he now felt safe and he was reunited with Doreen.

The remainder were feeling drowsy and as the suits were quite comfortable and gave a definite feeling of security, they did not feel inclined to strip off and don pyjama's, although they had been brought with them by the ever practical wives. The 'rests', as the Visitors called them, were found to be extremely comfortable and it was not long before all were asleep.

Adam's sleep was more like catnapping and he opened his eyes regularly, each time doubt arose as to whether he was dreaming, imagining or actually experiencing this extraordinary event. He noticed that the light, which had no determinate source, had become subdued and Adam considered the Visitors to be watching them or was it that it was an intelligent light source. We have security lights that come on if someone is detected by the beam he thought. What would his grandfather have made of those he wondered? He considered 100 years back, what a difference that period made to us he thought. If these Visitors were only 100 years ahead, their world would baffle us. Who knows how many years ahead they may be? Maybe they just developed more quickly and are not an older culture at all. Maybe the physics of their world are different from our own. So many possibilities rushed through his mind and he felt the adrenaline flow with the excitement of the possibility of being able to meet and communicate with people of another world –with so much to share with one another.

He saddened a little when he considered what had happened in our own past, when more advanced cultures - by technological measure perhaps - met with natives of other lands. If the Visitors are like ourselves, he thought, maybe we should take our chances with the trees. He had a feeling however that these Visitors were so advanced that the fear and greed that possessed our own kind had been overcome or perhaps never existed. The Visitors had little to fear, he thought, if they could avoid our fighters so easily. Yet our ancestors also had little to fear from most natives they came across. Unless, of course, they were isolated from their technology or by superior numbers. Then, there was much to fear because of their initial superior approach and greedy nature. A few missionaries ended up in the pot, but generally speaking those who went in peace were better off and Christianity became widespread and still remains so, whereas colonisation has not lasted unless beneficial to the native peoples. Lessons hard learned and only lately being heeded by the world at large. Perhaps too late he pondered.

Whilst man's thoughts were on other men and their possessions and land, the natural world around them - that they took so much for granted - had weapons in its armoury, never dreamed of by man. These weapons were being prepared, to eradicate what nature had come to identify as a parasite which endangered the entire planet with it's selfish behaviour.

70

As Adam napped and pondered alternately, the light increased in intensity as a new Earth day had begun. "What will today bring" said Adam to himself looking around to see if anyone else was awake yet.

Charley sensed sleeping time was over and heard, or sensed that Adam was awake and stood up off the floor and stretched before moving towards him. Jane also stirred and realised where she was with a start.

"Morning Dad, morning Charley" and Charley responded by trotting over and licking the hand that she extended towards him.

"Can I come with you if you take him for another walk Dad?"

"Better tell someone else before we do" said Adam.

Eddy was awake before long and father, daughter and family dog faded away. They arrived in the field behind their home where they often took the dog for a romp in the summer months. It was very warm and the sun was shinning like a summer's day. In fact that's just what it was, as the scene they were part of, was a day in June that they both remembered. Now they knew it to be a replay from their memories with themselves superimposed. Adam realised that the scene was slightly different somehow than he remembered it and studied the setting in great detail. He soon realised that the familiar things that he observed were larger than he knew them to be.

The penny dropped with a weird feeling of disbelief and wonderment. The scene he was looking at was the product of *Jane's* mind not his own. They could not *both* co-ordinate in different scenes so a single scene was created for them by one mind. This seemed to suggest that Jane's mind was the stronger or more relevant for the situation. Adam looked at Charley and wondered what his perspective was. He must think he's an Irish wolfhound, for his viewpoint would be a metre higher than normal. Perhaps it's different for him Adam thought and passed it off, as he enjoyed the pleasant warmth and view of the trees in full bloom. Charley ran around chasing insects for ten minutes perfectly adapted to his surroundings. When they looked at each other he surmised that they were looking at one another in reality and therefore relative perspectives were maintained. The backdrop supplied by Jane was the falsity, and the rest of the scene for that matter. They were back before anyone else but Eddy was aware they had gone.

Adam began to think about his employees. They would be preparing for a day's work as normal and then he realised it was Sunday. A more eventful weekend than either he or any of the others with him had ever experienced. With more to come as he was soon to find out.

The two women awakened to the rest watching them. "What are you staring at" said Jenny.

"Some people can sleep anywhere, eh Eddy?"

Imagination took care of all their morning needs, including the provision of a breakfast choice from a dispenser in the wall, which appeared with a little thought from Eddy. The wall space seemed adequate for the number of facilities it seemed to contain, indeed they soon discovered certain things appeared where others had previously been displayed. These Visitors were indeed master spacesavers.

The screen again came to life after they had breakfasted, Gold with a serious look on his face wished them all a good day, and hoped that they had rested well.

"We have a historic day in front of us and I hope you will be prepared to give your all for your fellow kind. Adam, would you and Jane come with the representative that will call for you. He will be Red our communications officer. There will be an information exchange in the room where you met yesterday. Escorts will collect you shortly, we have little time to spare."

The communication was polite but curt and to the point and sounded extremely ominous. Red duly arrived, his voice identical to Gold's. "Mr Briant, you and your daughter come with me without delay.

"Where are you taking them?" said Jenny looking worried.

"They are to come of their own free will," said Red.

"Suppose they don't want to go" said Jenny.

"Then they will remain here" replied Red.

"And suppose we want to go home?"

"Then you go home!" said Red "But you must decide quickly, we need to act without delay."

"We will go with him," said Adam persuasively. "We must help them to help us."

Jane needed no such persuasion; she was ready to go. They followed Red through the corridors to a room much smaller than the one they had come from. Gold and Silver were sitting by a circular table, as with the other table there was no apparent support, just the usual beam seat.

"Will you sit down" said Gold, and they all sat, equally spaced around the table. Gold continued to do all the talking, "Adam, we have the transmitter, your Pope has the receiver and Jane here has the interface. We need Jane's special mental abilities to make the required communications link. Red can transmit and receive but needs a human interface to interpret and relay. Do you understand?"

They both nodded in affirmation, their mouths slightly opened in surprise and awe at the possibility of being in contact with the Pope.

"We must begin immediately" said Red, sounding exactly like Gold in terms of voice but harsher and more direct in tone and intimation.

"No time like the present" said Jane excitedly.

"If everyone is ready then let us begin" said Gold.

"If everyone is sitting comfortably then I'll begin" said Jane with a laugh and a giggle.

"Jane be serious!" Adam snapped more through nervousness than anger.

All but Red and Jane left the table. Adam being beckoned away by Gold as they withdrew to the wall of the room.

"Concentrate on what you know the Pope to look like and his personality as you perceive it. Think into the man's thoughts, his essence, his being." He then went quiet in obvious concentration, pointing his thoughts through one narrow channel. Jane was less dynamic in her manner, sitting serenely with her eyes closed and a most appropriate angelic look on her face, with an air of subservience quite suited to an audience with the Holy Father.

There was complete silence for the next 10 minutes. The expressions of the two changed from time to time as with people in conversation. Then suddenly Jane burst into tears and dropped her head to her hands on the table. Adam could not contain himself and rushed forward to comfort his daughter.

"What's happening" he shouted, "what has happened Janey?"

"Its OK Dad, I'm OK!"

"He's so sad, so sad!" Red spoke, as all returned to join the two at the table. "He knows, he already knows that a great disaster is about to overtake the whole of humanity. He has been informed by other sources that our attempts to prevent it are to fail."

The meeting, announced earlier was duly held in the discussion room. All were in attendance, except for five of the crew who were otherwise engaged in the running the ship's systems.

Gold again took the chair. His address to the gathering was to be momentous. He was to tell the meeting things that they would have preferred not to hear. They were to be the last generation of humans to inhabit the Earth for the foreseeable future.

Chapter 11

Gold sat solemnly at the discussion table. "I have to tell you that reports from around your world have told of death on a large scale in many areas of rainforest. Animal and human casualties are growing in number in the path of prevailing winds. People are also reported to have been poisoned by fruits of the trees. Our other 11 ships are at present holding position and are communicating as we are. We regret our failure to prevent this disaster, as we said earlier we are not infallible and we are not gods. We do however intend to do what we can to conserve your kind and prevent its extinction. We would ask your co-operation in this task, as this is the reason for you being brought here. You are all safe with us, but what we ask of you will incur risk to your own survival."

There was a short silence as they digested the incredible announcement. None had experienced the announcement of world war, but this was what they likened to the present situation.

"What is it that you ask of us" said Adam seeming to pick up their own style of speaking.

"You will be required to collect the best of your kind and guide them to the pick up areas which we will designate. You will be landed in your own town area and due to the special properties of your suits, you will find it possible to leave the ground for brief periods. This will allow you to lift anyone who may not be able to make it on their own. By lifting them into the beam of light they can be brought aboard. Also because of your suits you will be located by our sensors and brought back to the ship even though you may be out of the beam. Pagers will be attached to your sleeves and with one touch on the sensor you will be brought back."

"The children will not be expected to go but any that wish to go with their parents and parents that wish them to go will be free to do so. You will be at risk, as they are, and some of you may perish."

"What about our friends and relations?" someone said.

"We will do what we can within our remit," said Gold, "but I'm afraid we cannot be more specific than the situation allows. If your relatives are in the drop area and satisfy the prime selection requirement then you may rescue them, but no special assignment will be allowed."

"What prime selection requirement" asked the questioner."

"Your dispatch guide will tell you in due course. Indicate if you do not wish to partake and you will stay on board and come to no harm."

The mother with the baby raised her hand and no one else.

"We would not expect it of you, you and your baby will be safe with us." said Gold. As he scanned around the table, there were no other hands raised. "I see we have chosen well - so be it."

The last thing that Gold said knocked Adam back almost as much as the announcement. It was, "You will need to be brave and quick, Gods speed to you all."

The other Visitors guided the groups to dispatch areas.

"A fine kettle of fish this is" said Eddy to Adam. "You know the way things are working out, if this is Armageddon, we are doing the angels' work!"

"Well you're blowing your trumpet too soon" said Doreen "We haven't done anything yet, and I hope we don't become fallen angels. I'm scared," she added in a lower tone.

"We must work together as a team" said Adam as they reached an area of the ship they had not seen before.

Meanwhile, on Earth, the news, which had been withheld for some time by governments for fear of panic, had leaked. Parts of the world were already on the streets in panic and demanding that something be done by the military, the government... anyone.

This was particularly pronounced where actual contact had been made with the dust. Bodies were scattered around, frozen into grotesque shapes with horrifying distorted faces as they died in obviously agonising pain. Some had been spared, as the winds swirled and veered. The thick brown dust having reaped a swathe of death, searched elsewhere for victims.

Some sought shelter inside and died under tables and blankets having been unable to find the protection they sought. Doors and windows were barricaded to no avail. Worse still were the partially affected, who cried out for death to take them and so escape the agony that they were suffering. Some committed suicide by throwing themselves from bridges and buildings. The populations of the countryside made tracks for the towns and cities, thinking that the scarcity of trees would mean less poisonous dust. However, as winds blew, so the dust was carried as seed from nettles in late summer, but reaching out over great distances, starting from a greater height and being of a lighter strain. This was the seed of death for humanity, so that the world of nature should survive.

Self defence is recognised, even by man, as mitigation for slaughter of his own kind. How much more so to rid nature of a parasite that endangered the whole. Looked at from the rest of the world's point of view of course. In the main Man however would seem to think that he is the proprietor rather than a caretaker. Perhaps an asset stripper rather than a manager. Maybe he thought he was superior to all else and therefore entitled to do, as was his wont? Whatever he thought, or thinks, today is to be his last day on Earth! Or is it?

Back in the Visitor's ship preparations were under way for an evacuation of some of the oxygen breathing life. Some of the twelve ships had been allocated to animal life, as the Visitors were here to help them too.

Major cities were chosen by the craft dedicated to human salvation, due to the high concentration of numbers and lower concentration of the poison. The Visitors were however aware of the countries, cities and towns that had environmental concern and had done something about it. This was one of their selection criteria, for if they were to perpetuate the human race they wanted the best specimens. This sounds harsh but it was logical. Suppose you owned two dogs, one of which had continually bitten you, and one that had been your friend and bitten only intruders. If you were able to save only one from a blazing house, which one would *you* choose?

The Visitors did have some knowledge of the people of Earth in their databases. These information records were quite extensive and they were able to extract data extremely quickly. This information was used to determine 'targets for salvation', as they phrased it.

Homer City was this ship's first target, just a hop away from where they were. The white suited people were issued with headgear that included communications and air supply, this could hardly be seen other than when the light reflected from it.

Doreen commented that Eddy now had the halo to go with the trumpet. "An unlikely angel if ever there was one" muttered Eddy. "You know Adam" he continued "with all these clones of you about, I now understand the phrase 'too many chiefs and not enough Indians'."

"Just checking you're not clocking on for someone else." retorted Adam.

The tension was rising regardless of the banter as the time of departure approached. The group of five was assembled together in the departure room to which their guide had brought them. Charley had been left in the discussion room with one of the guides who also looked after the woman with the baby.

The guide with Adam's group asked if all were comfortable with their suits and headgear. The guide then carried out a series of tests of the communicators and a scan for the sealing integrity of the suits. Eddy's halo headgear required a slight adjustment.

"My halo's slipping already Dor" said Eddy.

His communicator obviously worked because Doreen replied in a flash "Well at least it'll stop you blowing that trumpet."

"Raise your hand if you can hear me" said their guide, 'Blue'. Five hands were raised simultaneously. He then asked each in turn to say "yes I can!" An American amongst the group responded "affirmative!" Each transmitter and receiver was therefore confirmed.

"When you come into contact with a suitable person, an Aura of white light will appear around that person, this is created by your headgear which has a sensor to detect the correct data. Avoid anyone that does not show this Aura. If such a person tries to detain you, face that person directly, extend your arm or arms palms towards them and you will have no further trouble. Collect the people with an Aura that you come across and direct them to the War Memorial in the main town square. That is where you will find yourselves when you transport. We will bring you back after 15 minutes."

When Blue was sure that all was in order, he walked to the wall and as he did so a green light appeared and he turned and said, "raise your hands when you're ready." All five raised their hands and the lift feeling returned. Before they could lower their hands they found themselves standing in the familiar town centre.

By now it was mid-day and the town clock was striking 12 o'clock. The 12th hour had arrived. Others in the group had been landed in various parts of town. All, being locals, knew the town well - one good reason for their choice. The next 15 minutes were to prove crucial to the future of human kind. The race was on!

Chapter 12

The five briefly looked at one another and then looked around the square. Few people could be seen, as television and radio were announcing a state of Worldwide emergency, telling people to stay indoors and to seal all doors and windows. This was to be detrimental to the rescue mission in one way, but meant that fewer people were panicking on the streets. Those that would be on the streets were, in the main, the young and fit but many would be beyond rescue, out of sight indoors.

A group of teenagers were listening to a radio in the corner of the square. When they saw the five figures in white seemingly materialise in the middle of the square, they gestured and most ran off in fright but three remained and ventured towards the group. The five looked in the direction of the teenagers and all were startled by what they saw. The one leading the three approached warily, but the two following were illuminated in a dim but unmistakable white glow. The five remembered their briefing and as the leader without the light approached they could see that he was brandishing a knife and showing it to the group in a threatening manner. Adam stepped forward raising his arm as instructed with the palm of his hand towards the youth. Immediately the unfortunate lad stopped in his tracks frozen in his final gesture, after a short time it was obvious that he was not going to move any further. The two others turned on their heels and ran, still appearing to glow slightly and although Adam called out to them, they were not going to stop until they were well away from these 'aliens', as the five must have been perceived.

Eddy cracked that this one had not eaten his porridge this morning, as he looked over the new statue in the Town Square and removed the knife from its hand. "Won't need that again my lad" he said as he tossed it down a grid.

"We are scaring more than we are saving" said Jenny.

They noticed a light, although it was broad daylight, glowing in the arcade behind the Memorial. Walking over to the source of the light they found a vagrant asleep, with a bottle in his hand. "An unlikely desirable" said Jane.

"Never judge by appearance" said her mother. As they moved a cardboard cover a flood of light seemed to emit from this bedraggled figure such that they were dazzled for a moment. Then they noticed the string of medals hanging from his tattered raincoat and Adam realised that the brightness of the light was not due to this person's worldly possessions but to his inner values.

"Lets get him to the pick up area" said Adam

"He smells!" said Jane screwing up her nose.

"Obviously of the right stuff "said Eddy "I'll take his feet".

As they carried him to the Open square, his weight seemed to lighten and they found themselves holding just a tattered raincoat but without the medals.

"I guess they thought the medals were more part of the man than the raincoat" said Adam.

"Lets go, 5 minutes have passed and we only have one" said Doreen.

A voice they recognised as Gold's was heard by all to say that they had managed to communicate with the world leaders and that they had agreed to broadcast over radio and television. The leaders had agreed to inform all, to co-operate with any people fitting your description and that they are official representatives of WorldWide Research Corporation. To say that they were there to save them from death would cause mayhem, but this way at least may prevent them from attacking them or simply running away in fear.

"By the way," said Gold, "we have the two teenagers that ran away so your score is three but please hurry."

"That's the first time I've heard him say please "said Jenny. Not expecting Gold to hear let alone apologise at being a slow learner. "Oop's!" said Jenny "my big mouth."

" Move towards the residential areas" said Gold "that's where most of the people are."

"Down Sutton Lane," said Doreen "there are a lot of children in that area, around St. Joseph's School."

Being Sunday they knew that they would not be in school. Not that they would be anyhow by now, but the area was heavily populated. Gold's voice returned warning that the prevalent wind was bringing poison towards the south of the city triggering other trees and plants as it reached them. A man and a woman opened the door as the five passed their house.

They called out. "Are you the people to help us?" Adam saw that they had the necessary Aura and therefore replied. "Yes come with us." The two joined the group.

"Where are the children," said Jenny.

"There are two with the family at number 5" said the woman.

"Do you know them" said Jenny.

"Yes, they are friends of ours, please can you help them?"

"We will try" said Jenny. "Will you fetch them?"

When they came from their home they were obviously afraid and cowered away until Doreen, Jenny and Jane knelt down to say hello. Fortunately all had the Aura shown by the sensors in the halo. They had not moved far from the square and Adam asked the women to escort them back to the War Memorial. Eddy and he would carry on with Jane and find more.

The group moved off with the children who were aged 3 and 5 years both with bright Auras. As they were to find out, nearly all children under 5 had Auras. They did not come across any without and they were grateful for that. There were faint screams from the south of the city and some vehicles could be heard with screeching tyres. The five knew what was happening.

"We must hurry," said Eddy it's getting close."
Gold intervened, "you have only 5 minutes left, however you do not need to return to the square. We will bring you in, just hold on to the people that you collect. You don't need to touch all but each must touch one another to form a connection up to a maximum of ten inclusive."

"You mean hold hands in a circle" said Adam impatiently.

"I believe I do" he responded.

They continued to walk down the road and felt eyes watching them from the houses they passed. Most were still to afraid to come out and curtains twitched in windows. Adam beckoned to a family he saw looking through a half-opened door. The Auras were obvious and they began to approach, once started they got faster until they were nearly into a run. It was a family of six , five with various Auras but unfortunately the last one out was a man who had no light Aura. The three looked at one another and back at the man, as the man was hanging back he got separated from the rest and then, realising he was being left behind, started desperately to try and catch up. Adam quickly intervened and raised his hand. The man stopped before the affect, whatever it was, took place, and he ran back into the house and shut the door.

"What's wrong with him?" said one of the children.

"Who is he?" asked Eddy.

"He asked us to allow him in to see the news announcements" replied the father of the family. "What's he up to? I didn't like the look of him much."

"Whatever forget it, it doesn't matter much now, lets get going." said Adam, conscious of the time left and the few people they had collected. They could now only collect two more before time ran out.

"Stay close to us whilst we pick up two more."

A group of people came running at full speed down the road as though the devil himself was after them and when they saw the three in white, gave them a wide berth shouting "get away, people are being killed it's here" as they went. Some were carrying items of various types from fur coats to portable TV sets. It was not clear if the items belonged to them. Only one of the seven had a light Aura if that was any indication. They may have been more interested in the opportunities provided to steal and so missed the broadcast that told of the collectors.

"The devil too has angels" said Jane.

One of the children on hearing this asked, "are you angels then?"

"No we're not angels" said Eddy, "but we can help you."

A family came from a house further down the road, a man a woman and a small boy. The group moved towards them and as they came near the three collectors saw two Auras. Only the man was dark. "Oh my goodness" said Adam.

"No time for questions" said Eddy "allow me." He stepped forward and held up his hand in front of the man. The man froze in his tracks with a questioning look fixed on his face. The woman and boy also stopped, "What have you done!" said the woman.

"No time to explain now" said Adam "please join us if you want your son and yourself to survive." The mention of her son surviving was enough to make the women leave her husband if that was what he was.

No sooner had the pair joined the group when Gold's voice announced "time has elapsed join hands now."

The three asked the group to hold hands in a circle and as soon as the last hand was joined the whole group rose into the air. "Hold on tight everyone" shouted Adam, as much surprised as the rest of them.

"Don't worry" ('fear not', updated in his vocabulary) said Gold "we have you now." They were flying through the air and could see the vision of disaster being acted out below them as people fled and bodies lay on the ground. Fires had broken out, vehicles had crashed, a cloud of brown dust, which looked like smoke, billowed from trees and floated on the wind like the plague on Egypt. The three recognised the square directly below them and in a flash they appeared back in the departure room on the ship. The children were crying loudly from the experience and their mothers comforted them.

Blue escorted them to the discussion room to make them comfortable.

"We must go back" said Adam. The other four agreed.

"You can't go back to Homer" said Blue "it's too late".

"Then let's go where we aren't too late" said Eddy.

"We are already in position over Compton" said Blue.

"Why can't you just beam them onboard" said Jenny. Practically minded as ever.

"That is not possible" said Blue "They have to come of their own volition or be identified as suitable by yourselves, by the light Aura that only you can invoke, as their own kind.

"We're wasting time," said Adam "explain later, let's go."

They repeated the process three more times, never able to stay more than 15 minutes due to the rapid spread of the triggering mechanism. Then it was too late for any more sorties, the human race and in fact all oxygen breathing life on Earth had been extinguished.

Chapter 13

Although it was less than a couple of hours since they started their rescue quest, all were drained both physically and emotionally. They were back onboard their lifeboat - for that is what it felt like. Even if it was an alien vessel it was their only means of survival.

Their ordeal was not yet over. Gold requested Adam and Jane to join him in the room that they had used before - when communicating with the Pope. Red was again there and Gold explained that help was now needed to rescue the passengers and crews of ships and air liners. As yet these had not been affected but they were aware that they had no ports or air ports at which to disembark, without meeting the deadly dust. Theirs would be a delayed death but just as inevitable, as the dust spread to the ocean areas. In the case of the aircraft, the obvious crash as they ran out of fuel.

Red and Jane together, the Visitors believed, could identify desirable targets and distinguish them from the undesirable. Of course they could only reach a fraction of the total in that situation but they should go ahead anyway.

Adam expressed concern that Jane was tired, but Jane, with maturity beyond her years, shrugged at her father saying she felt all right and must try to help. He agreed.

Jane sat at the small round table, as before, opposite Red. The wall to their right cleared to a window and they looked out into a blue sky and below to the left was a white jumbo jet. The objective was, by the power of thought transfer, to identify dark Auras as these were usually in the minority, and having done so transfer onboard all others. This proved to be impossible.

The problem lay in the fact that those on board the aircraft were aware of the happenings on the ground. Air traffic control had relayed news of the situation, warning the crew not to land, and then died. The flight crew had then felt it necessary to inform all on board of the problems preventing them from landing. The resulting mass of anxiety permeating the aircraft made adequate communication of the type required impossible and their inevitable fate was sealed.

Red and Jane then scanned the ocean for shipping where they discovered a passenger liner steaming at full speed. As the pair prepared to contact the passengers Jane shuddered with anguish and broke off her mental search. "They're dead!" she said.

"They can't be, try again" said Red. "You would not get through if they were all dead, you must have communicated with someone"

"Just a minute" said Adam "she's had enough."

"It's OK Dad," she said "he's right, I was looking through someone's eyes, there were bodies everywhere, it was horrible."

" We must try again we may save someone."

"Let's do it Red." By now Jane was accustomed to the fact that all the people around her looked like her father, except for their suit colour. Yet she knew she could identify each individual now even if they did wear the same colour. Looks are easier to copy than personality she thought.

They went to it again and this time she managed to stay with her contact. There were only four people left alive and they had on diver's masks and were breathing from oxygen tanks from the medical room. She detected light Auras from all and sighed with relief at the thought of not having to identify anyone to leave behind. She had picked up from their thoughts that they had trees and large plants onboard which had started giving off poison. They were aware also of what was happening on land but before they could get to the plants to throw them overboard it was already happening and most were overcome. On hearing that the light Aura was present in all four, Gold immediately gave orders to transport them aboard and it was done.

Jane slumped and wiped her face with the back of her hand. "We got them Red, you and I got them. What's next?"

"No more" said Adam "You've done enough for one young lady."

She knew that when he called her young lady he was either very annoyed with her or very pleased, she felt it should be the latter.

"What now?" asked Adam.

"We have now saved all we can" said Gold.

"Can they all live indefinitely on this ship" said Adam.

"No" replied Gold "We now have to return to our Mothership."

"Mothership? You mean you have a larger ship than this?"

"Yes indeed was the reply, all twelve cruiserships are carried by our Mothership. We are expected to rendezvous with her in ten minutes time."

"You can observe it from here if you wish."

They took seats at the table with Red and Jane. "What are you going to do with the people you saved? There must be hundreds."

"1502 in total," said Gold "and an assortment of 50 animals. A pitifully small number but with God's help enough."

"I didn't see God doing much down there" said Adam.

"He was there!" said Gold. "Most of those that died are now in his domain."

"And the rest?" Adam questioned.

"Hell of course," was Gold's unexpected response. "Look we are approaching the Mothership."
The transparent wall gave a view that astonished all the humans on board. What all could see at this moment was a ship that all but defied description.

"Three miles long and half a mile wide" declared Gold with pride. The ship they were approaching dwarfed the twelve cruiseships that were as specks by comparison. Black in colour with no markings and a rough looking outer skin like elephant hide.

The cruisers approaching broke vee formation to single file, the ship that Adam and the rest were on took fifth place in the file, as number one swung around to align with the end of the Mothership and disappeared into the end which had opened like a camera iris. As Adam's ship took its turn to align for entry, they saw into the vessel. This was illuminated with a reddish diffused light with bright blue spots which each cruiser in turn aimed for, the lights extinguishing one by one as each came to rest as smoothly as though on water. Adam and Jane were asked to re-join the others who were now in the discussion room.

Jane saw the woman with the boy whose father was not brought up, and wondered why they were not complaining. She would find out later.

Jenny wanted to know what the pair of them had been doing, and was told by Adam that Jane had been helping to save lives and she should be proud of her daughter - she was a heroine.

Some of the humans where in shock and some were distraught. However all were in awe of the technology of these Visitors that had saved their lives. But the question in everyone's mind was 'what happens now?' 'What are they going to do with us?' They were to disembark into the Mothership before the answers were forthcoming.

Chapter 14

As they approached the interior they saw that other types of craft could be seen, suspended above them. These were silver disc type craft, which had semi-spherical pods on their underside. The typical flying saucer as described by George Adamski in the 50's and many others since. "Scoutships" said Adam under his breath. This was obviously a hanger deck, in a very literal sense.

These Visitors may not have communicated fully for thousands of years but they have been with us over the years. Keeping an eye on us. The question is why? They may be about to find out.

"We are to disembark as soon as possible" announced Gold. "Please be patient, meanwhile if you require any service at all, such as toilets, food or drink or anything else, ask the people in white who are your own kind. Without these people we would not have been able to rescue you. We are thankful to them and you should be too. They risked their lives to save yours, and I regret to inform you that one of their number lost their life in the process. Her name was Amy Jones."

Jane immediately recognised the name it was the schoolteacher she had recognised earlier. When she broke into tears, her mother and father were puzzled until he explained.

Gold continued. "She will not be forgotten on this disastrous day for your kind, she was killed whilst rescuing a family who were being attacked by others of your kind for their belongings. The family are amongst you, thanks to her efforts and I would ask you all to remember with pride what she and the others did for their fellow beings on this day." With that he bowed his head and stepped down from the gantry from where he was addressing the 150 or so people.

As Jane's parents comforted her, Eddy remarked how unexpected to find that an alien race believed in God.

"It may not be our God" said Jenny. "Most people have a god but many different gods can be found."

Adam remembered the comment Gold had made earlier. "Only one God", he said, "I have a feeling that it is the same one. Remember when he said 'as it is written', when I asked him who we should condemn to death by not allowing them to come. I think their God is our God too".

"Hope so," said Jenny in that off-handed manner she had when discussing such matters. "It would make me feel a lot better."

Doreen who had been very quiet added. "We certainly came close to finding out today".

"I think we did " said Eddy in a doleful manner.

"So many people died today but to have known just one personally seems to make it so much worse" said Jane.

"I don't want to dwell on it" said her father "but a whole lot more have gone than we realise yet. 1500 or so of the whole population of Earth is a minute proportion." All of them went silent in respectful remembrance of family and friends, and the rest of the human race, not forgetting all other oxygen dependent creatures.

The assembly was ushered to a large doorway that had opened up in the wall of the ship, and they walked across a level ramp about 10 metres wide, which took them from the hanger deck to the living quarters of the Visitors. Eyes bulged as they took in the awesome sights before them.

Some youngster was heard to say, "Is this heaven Mummy." But even more surprising was the mothers reply. "Yes darling, I think it might be; wipe your mouth dear."

The inner area of the Mothership was so large that it appeared to be an open area of beautiful landscape with waterfalls, pathways lined with plants of incredible colour and variety and trees of a type they didn't recognise. They were a bit wary of the trees considering what they had just gone through.

"Don't fear any plants here," announced Gold, "they are not of your planet and are perfectly safe. Like yours used to do, they provide our air to breathe, but we are able to monitor and communicate with them. They are our friends, and we are theirs". The emphasis on 'we' seeming to indicate the difference between their race and ours.

There was bright light like brilliant sunlight but no sun or source of light was apparent. The pathways were wide and golden yellow in colour, small vehicles could be seen flying around, and on closer inspection were seen to be just boards like skateboards with small figures on them which they took for children due to their size. Due to the distance, they could not make out detail and none came close to the survivors.

There was a warm gentle breeze and insects could be heard and seen flitting about. Large butterfly like insects fluttered from flower to flower.

"I can understand that child's assumption" said Doreen.

"Are we dead?" said Eddy "it's like a dream of paradise" and he pinched himself.

They were being kept in their respective groups as they disembarked. As each group viewed the others they knew that the sum of all the groups was what was left of the whole human race. 1502 people would not fill the end paddock of the average football ground. The survival of the human race depended on these few, for which the full implications had not yet been digested.

They were directed to dome shaped buildings, which had doors like the space cruisers, not detectable until used and then becoming undetectable once more after use. The groups stayed apart for the time being. They were welcomed to the Space Home Craft Atlantis. One of five such homes they were told, by Gold. As you will have guessed, he was personnel officer for their group. Skirting the walls of the room were the other Visitors from the cruiser they had just left. All eleven - the first time that they had seen them all together. Each had a different colour suit as they had been told but not really noticeable unless close to. Adam felt uneasy looking at twelve replicas of himself.

Gold sensed his unease and revealed that, now they were back home, the Visitors would be reverting to their normal appearance at the conclusion of the meeting to introduce the guests formally to their hosts. He repeated that they were pleased to have their neighbours here in their home for a while, but regretted that they could not prevent what had happened.

However what has come to pass has past and they must look to the future. They must perpetuate the human race as its potential as a full member of the inhabited planet society was expected and awaited with interest.

He continued "there are many planets out there with intelligent life. As each reached an acceptable level of development it would be welcomed to join the society and share beneficial knowledge. You were so close, but all is not lost, you may still go on and achieve your rightful position in the society. There was proof of that in your actions today, indeed in excess by the demonstration of selflessness shown by Amy Jones and may I also mention Jane Briant for her exceptional abilities without which we would not have been able to do as much as we did."

Jane blushed uncontrollably and looked down at the floor.

"You also have the dark side in some of your kind and they have held you back for centuries. That is not unique to humans, but enough, we have experienced too much to dwell on such things. We have brought you here to unite you all and to transport you to an artificial world until your own world is again ready to accept you."

"Where is this artificial world?" said Adam.

"It will be released into the asteroid belt between Mars and Jupiter. It could be deployed as a satellite of Earth, except for the fact that it would be vulnerable. In the asteroid belt it will be hidden from long distance scans."

Adam and the rest still had not absorbed the first part. 'Deployed from where?' Then they realised that this artificial world was here, on board this gigantic mobile home, like a tent carried for the children in a camper.

"How much space will we have?" a woman asked.

"There will be adequate room for you to develop and multiply" said Gold. "The diameter of the microworld is just 1/4 mile until deployed. It then is extended all around to an irregular shape to maintain a low profile amongst the asteroids, it will expand to suit your needs up to a length of 1 mile."

"Why the camouflage?" asked Adam who was becoming the naturally evolved spokesman for the humans.

"There are undesirable types in the universe," said Gold. "As I said the darker side is not unique to humans. But you must be optimistic to succeed. Now before you meet us as we really are, whatever your impressions, remember we are your allies and are trying to save your kind from extinction." With that he gestured to the other eleven crew to join him.

The tension was high like a magician working up to his final illusion. They stood a metre apart and touched their left breast with their right hands, which made them look like Americans swearing allegiance. Maybe they were doing something similar, but the effect was to create a haze around each as their features became obliterated. They shrank down to a metre in height and half their original width. As the haze cleared, the features were completely rearranged, their skin was now grey their eyes larger much larger and their major feature, deep blue and oval rather than round, no hair, sharp pointed chins and holes for ears. The group of humans looked around and muttered to one another.

"I hope we don't appear offensive or frightening in anyway" said Gold still wearing his suit that still appeared tailor made. "We have had many years to become accustomed to yourselves, we must be very different to you. We are aware that your kind feels uneasy with different appearances and that it can cause aggression in you."

"You do us an injustice" said Adam "we have progressed a great deal lately. You have proved your worthiness as our friends and indeed saviours, and we are very pleased to have met you however you look."

"Thank you Adam," said Gold. "I must say we are not to keen on your hair, it looks a little animal like to us, but we have got used to it, and still would not want to see you become extinct. We share a common God regardless of your religion, or lack of it," and he looked towards Eddy as though he knew Eddy's thoughts. "We will talk again later as you will all now meet up in the missions room. Will you follow us now please?" and the door swished open at their approach.

The group filed out and as they went saw the other groups also following twelve aliens looking just like their twelve. The aliens appeared like children now that they were back in their own form and only a metre high. The group now realised that the figures they could see on skate boards where aliens not children, they still wondered however if they were alien children. As one came close they could see that the board was in fact suspended about 50 cms above the path but also had wheels and a curious trailing tail which reached the path. They continued to a larger dome where one group was already going in and looking back to see the others following. As they caught up a man at the back of the group in front turned and commented "not exactly handsome are they!" With little time to reflect Doreen responded "not exactly grateful are you!" The man turned to the front suitably embarrassed. "He's nervous" Adam said. "Some people have to make those sort of comments to feel part of the group." "Well now he knows the sort of group he's part of." Gold who was at the front of the group, turned to

Adam and asked, "What is handsome?" It seemed very strange to Adam and the others, for this alien to be speaking and sounding like Gold as the clone of Adam. Almost as strange as talking to himself for the first time - but he was soon to become accustomed.

Chapter 15

The fact that the aliens were so small detracted from their authority for a while. However it did not take long for their real power to show, and the remnants of humanity recognised their superior stage of evolutionary development.

The survivors were shown areas of recreation where real and holograph technology combined to create sports and pastimes to human taste. Sailing on an indoor ocean with palm tree islands and white sand beaches. Ski-ing on beautiful slopes and ski lifts. Nightclubs, amusements, tennis courts, swimming, films - virtually anything they desired.

A church was set up for their worship, and as a number of ordained men were amongst them there was no shortage of people to carry out the services. The aliens had their own sort of worship and practised it daily. They told the survivors that during the fall of man, as they phrased it, they had observed angels of God and the Devil at work and that even though the majority of people had died, heaven and hell still had plenty of capacity.

Their belief was that God made the universe, the Earth being one small planet could not fill but one tiny corner of heaven, or hell. Adam discussed such things with the aliens, for it seemed their knowledge of the subject was more detailed than his own. The aliens pointed out that they referred to themselves as Guardians. "Guardians from the planet Garden," Adam joked. The Guardians did not share the humour. "Humans from the planet Earth" they replied. "We are all creatures of God on the Homeship of the Guardians for the time being."

The oxygen content in the atmosphere of the Homeship had to be increased for the humans, it was necessary therefore to provide enriched oxygen in all domes used by them. This was not desirable for the Guardians and had to be adjusted which meant that the humans would get breathless in the open ship atmosphere if they stayed for too long or exerted themselves.

Meanwhile Charley was making himself at home and seemed to enjoy the new environment; there were other small dogs with which he exchanged barks and sniffs. There were also a number of cats, which caused the usual dog/cat conflicts. The accommodation was similar to that described on the cruiser ships but larger. Individual accommodation however, like the family home on Earth, was not provided, families shared large domes which housed up to twelve people, this number was common amongst the Guardian world and seemed to hold some significance not known to the humans.

The Guardians asked the humans to elect a council of communication with whom they would consult and confer over decisions. Jane was elected as one of the council even before her father, the words spoken of her by Gold had been taken to heart by the humans and she was looked on as a heroine by some, as was Amy Jones in their memory of that terrible day in September. Adam was elected leader of this council which consisted of twelve, four men, four women, and four children - two boys and two girls. This was all very democratic and provided for some interesting and sometimes loud discussions between themselves.

Meetings with the Guardians however always seemed quiet and respectful. These small statured but recognisably large brained thinking creatures had a way of inducing calm and common sense into their communications never becoming angry but insistent at times when they thought it for the good of the community as a whole.

The humans were informed that the journey to the asteroid belt would take 6 months. This was because the "Mothership", (as it was called when talking travel, or away from the ship in a scout or cruiser, and "Homeship" when at home in the ship), could not use intergalactic speed whilst in a solar system. They must however refuel whilst in the solar system. To do this they must journey towards the Sun to a distance that would bring them to the orbit of Mercury. Here they would take on energy from the Sun through the skin of the ship. This was the reason for it being the black and rough surface that it was. The surface area being increased by the roughness and the absorbency by the black colour. The radiation is absorbed through the skin and stored by batteries of cells throughout the inner skin. Three miles long and half a mile wide was a big surface area. The scouts and cruisers also tapped this energy whilst stowed in the hanger. It was energy utilised in a similar way to plant photo-synthesis. There were alternative energy sources however. Backup and auxiliary energy, such as gravitational fields of suns and planets, blackhole sling, solar winds and comet draught for example.

Passage through a blackhole by the way was not possible even with their advanced technology. Such obstacles had to be negotiated with great care, much like a whirlpool in a lake, but with expertise great velocity could be achieved by surfing the outer edges of these phenomenon. This was avoided except for special exploration voyages and only attempted by very brave and specialist members of the Guardian civilisation.

The trip to the sun and back would add another 6 months. In the total twelve months that it would take to get to the asteroid belt the Guardians would instruct and guide the humans in the ways of the artificial world. The humans were somewhat shaken by the news that the Guardians would be leaving as soon as the world was deployed. They had already formed a relationship and respect with these friendly aliens and a fear of being left alone nagged at the thoughts of many if not all the human survivors.

The journey to the sun was to begin as soon as the Mothership was prepared and the Guardians were busy moving about on their transport boards all around the ship, but mainly centred on the large domes near to the hanger area. An announcement was made over the intercom which said that they were about to get under way, orbital stationing anchors where at this moment being disengaged, and a request to remain stationary and seated during the initial acceleration period which would last for five minutes only.

There was a slight vibration through the floor that could be felt also in the walls, but nothing through the seat beams. Another announcement five minutes later declared that the ship was under way, and that normal activities could be resumed.

"Hardly worth telling us about" said Eddy.

"Nice to know what's happening though" replied Adam.

"Do you realise the significance of the event Eddy. "The last of the human race is leaving Earth, perhaps for ever."

A tear ran down Jane's cheek as she remembered her friends and relations and of course Amy Jones "I think we should have some sort of service" said Jenny to Adam.

They called a council meeting as soon as the Guardian representatives were available and agreement was soon reached that a service must be held. It was arranged to take place within a dome especially equipped for such services, the wall of which cleared to a screen or was it a window, it was impossible to tell. The view was spectacular. The Earth still large and taking up most of the viewing area, blue with wisps of feathery clouds, these however were tinged with brown instead of the clean white heavenly whisps that they remembered from photographs taken by the American space research programme.

"Like sand on the snow" said Eddy.

"Blood and sand on the snow" murmured Doreen.

A preacher named Brian officiated at a service that mourned the death of mankind on Earth, and asked God to help them survive the perils that may lie ahead, and thanked him for the Guardians who had plucked them from the jaws of death. He commented that they felt closer to him than ever in this environment and hoped that he would continue to look after them on their unexpected voyage. Amy Jones was commended to his care as one who gave her life so that others should partake in this voyage of survival. They, the few left to perpetuate humanity, must embody their spirit in the generations to come.

Amy Jones was to become a legend in the New World, along with others amongst these survivors. They had no way of knowing at this time, although they did sense that they were the seedcorn for the future humanity, if it were to survive.

The ship pulled away from the Earth, and they watched the Earth recede until it was just a bright spot in the sky. The view changed to another larger spot in the sky that was noticeably getting larger. This was Venus and they were heading towards its orbit. They could now see the Sun in the viewer.

"Should we be able to look directly at the Sun", asked Jane?

"It is a scanner picture, not a direct view, explained Adam.

"It does have a filter," said Gold, who was in attendance to show respect, "or you would suffer eye damage. The resolution of the scanner and viewer is good enough to do that, without the filter it would be close enough to the real thing to cause visual damage when focused on a sun. We, as I said before have two suns, the light emitted is greater than yours and nature has provided us with a natural filter. In bright light these automatically cover our eyes."

"Like built in sunglasses," said Jane "cool, can you show me."

"Afraid not" replied Gold "it works a little like the iris of your own eyes, we cannot operate them manually, in our case it is a film that covers rather than a variable aperture. It achieves the same objective. More than one way of skinning a dog, as your saying goes."

"I think you mean 'cat' sir" said Jane respectfully.

"Well," replied Gold "I did tell you that we are not infallible, but why would you want to skin a cat?"
"Or a dog!" said Jane.

"Quite!" said Gold, "but it is your expression, not ours." As he turned back to Adam. The features of the Guardians seemed not to allow for smiling, but Adam did notice a glint of amusement in the extremely expressive eyes.

The Mothership was gaining speed still and the trip to Mercury's orbit would take three months at solar system restricted speed. By the time they reached Venus's orbit they were at that maximum speed limit.

 "Are there interplanetary speed cops" asked Eddy.

The Guardians replied that there was an organisation that *was* similar to a police force. The reason for their speed restriction however was nothing to do with speed regulations but the practicalities of relatively confined space. A solar system they said can be disrupted by their secondary drive systems. It also takes a long period of sustained acceleration to achieve the secondary system top speeds. Then they would also require a great deal of space to decelerate.

"We're like a tanker in a canal" suggested Eddy.

"Possibly so," was the reply, but he had the feeling that they didn't really comprehend and were only being polite.

The humans and the Guardians were beginning to understand and get on well together by the time they approached Mercury. They took up orbit in diametric opposition to the planet so as to avoid any undesirable gravitational influence. The views they were seeing were unbelievable, displays of solar flares which threatened to engulf them or at least they thought so. Seas of fire, strange whirlpools of orange bubbling matter, not recognisable as molten rock or flames, seemingly a hybrid substance of gas and solid, maybe plasma. Whatever it was it raged violently as though in anger at being held by gravity and threshing to escape and be free. One day it would succeed and devour it's own children, it's planets and their residents. By that time man may be widespread or he may have been extinct for centuries. Maybe as of *this* century they thought - wondering at their own continued existence, for they were all that was left of mankind at this point in time.

They parked in orbit for a week (by Earth time), revolving like a chicken on a spit. There was some discomfort in the minds of the humans wondering how the hull could put up with the radiation of such large amounts of heat. In addition they were buffeted as though a hurricane was blowing outside, in fact something much worse was going on but the ship they were told had stabilisers to reduce the buffeting and they were 70% effective.

At last the refuelling was complete and the ship edged away comparatively slowly, the buffeting reduced and eventually died out altogether, and the humans metaphorically wiped their brows.

Doreen commented that it felt like the first lock she passed through on a canal cruising holiday they had taken two years ago. Adam asked how long the ship would now run before needing refuelling. He was told that if they were on an intergalactic voyage at full speed they could travel for twelve Earth years. It was in fact seven years since they last refuelled, travel around solar systems using Scoutships and cruisers etc., drained their fuel more quickly.
Glad you were with us said the Guardians, the feeling is mutual said the humans with a sigh of relief and a tongue in the cheek.

Chapter 16

Three more months passed and they were re-approaching Earth. Viewers were switched on and what they saw filled them with dread and sorrow, for the Earth was not recognisable, the blue planet was now the brown planet, it was completely covered and looked like a football on a muddy pitch in March.

"Maybe that's how it got the name Earth," commented Adam "it looks like earth now. Seen as it was, it could have been called 'Ocean' or 'Marina'. I wonder... he muttered."

"You wonder what?" said Eddy.

"Oh nothing," replied Adam "just dreaming again. We will be back some day!"

The Earth receded again and they gazed at it until it was just a speck on the Viewer. That was the last they ever saw of it - most of them through watery eyes. A great melancholy fell over the whole ship, a melancholy that was shared by the Guardians.

Three more months passed and preparations were underway on the artificial world carried at the opposite end of the ship to the hanger and great activity along the length of the ship.

Transporters were carrying equipment, personnel and supplies to the part of the ship that looked, at this stage like a spherical bulkhead, at the extreme end of the ship. On passing through the access doors it appeared much the same as the other parts of the ship but more compact. There was a hanger with six scout ships and six cruisers. The same plants and flowers including areas of food producing plants. The humans asked why these were needed when they had the ability to produce food by synthesis. The explanation was 'backup'. Everything they needed had to have an alternative in case of failure, they explained and some things had multiple alternatives. This seemed to be a major policy factor for the Guardians, which would stand the survivors in good stead.

They were approaching Mars in the ninth month and the red planet was like a marker buoy as they passed by. A million years or so ago, they were told, "there was an atmosphere on this planet and a civilisation with connections to Earth's Egyptian race. They fled to an outpost on a moon of Jupiter but then mysteriously disappeared between our visits, we never did find out why or were they went to. They also had connections with our own system but they were a mysterious secretive race who preferred to stay remote and guarded their secrets with great rigidity, even to the point of death, and beyond. One theory is that they all committed suicide to join their gods in the afterlife that they revered so much. However no trace was ever found of the bodies, only artefacts and buildings, of which most were transported to a memorial planet in the Catraya galaxy, although a few sculptures remain in respect for their home planet. We believe your probes detected one or more of these. There are more covered by the dust".

Could Big Ben, The White House, The Taj Mahal, end up in the Catraya galaxy, thought Adam? Mars receded as they passed and they were on their way to their destination amongst the asteroids.

112

At last they started to come across odd boulders and the speed of the ship was reduced to dead slow, power had been cut after leaving the orbit of Mars but still some reverse power was needed such was the momentum of a three mile long ship. The power field shields that extended for a kilometre all around the ship - like fendoffs - deflected smaller boulders. This protected the ship from meteor strikes which were normally quite small some even minute. Now, however, the asteroids were sometimes as large as a football pitch and avoidance was wiser when they reached this size, some of course where much larger and like small planets. It was not clear whether these were planets that never formed or ones which broke up, or even blew up. If the Guardians knew they were not letting on.

They came to a stop in the thick of it, and the view was something else. The Guardians were working like bees and the artificial asteroid or world as they referred to it was at last ready to go. A countdown began and scanners on the outside of the ship were adjusted to follow the deployment. It could have been described as the birth of their world to be.

The humans thought that they may board the world before deployment and be ejected with it. This was not the way the Guardians wanted it. Their way was to deploy and transfer personnel afterwards by scout or cruiser. It was a tense time for everyone by virtue of the sheer size of the project.

The countdown reached deployment -12 seconds and they were counted off just as our own space launches. 11, 10, 9, 8, 7, 6, 5, 4, 3, 2, 1, 0 a hissing noise followed by clanks and clicks as release mechanisms disengaged. Some watched from the final bulkhead windows as the spherical end of the world slipped away like the launch of some monster tanker. From the viewers it was like a large caterpillar giving birth, the world was spherical at this time, it emerged slowly into black space and then reflecting the light of the sun stood out in stark relief but grey in colour which would allow it to blend into its environment. As it cleared the tail of the Mothership the iris type door closed immediately and pressurisation was renewed to secure the rest of the Mothership.

The people behind the bulkhead turned their attention to the Viewers. As they watched, a metamorphosis began to take place and the spherical shape began to bulge and distort and spread to a larger volume - just like an inflatable liferaft. By the time it stopped it was twice the size it had been, irregular and indistinguishable from the other asteroids that they had seen on the approach. There were many different shapes and sizes and no better place to hide - but from whom or from what?

The Guardians called a meeting of all personnel and humans. The agenda consisted of the following,

1) Operational systems including manuals with computer translations.
2) Use of Scout and Cruisers.
3) Emergency Evacuation (using items in 2).
4) Expansion of living space if population increase requires it.
5) Energy conservation and backup generation systems.
6) Volunteer Guardians to stay and help.
7) Recommended activities.
9) Holographic recreation.
10) Departure of the Mothership.
11) Communications with Mothership.
12) Periodic return of Mothership.
Any further business?

Having discussed in some detail the items on the agenda the Guardians withdrew, wishing their wards God's protection, and good luck! It was with great surprise but delight that Adam discovered Gold was to be one of the two volunteers to stay behind, the other was Red the communications officer. The parting was made easier for Adam and his group due to this. Jane had a rapport with Red and was delighted to be able to continue her studies of telepathy that she had been working on with Red's help and guidance, he had become her mentor, and the two had made great leaps in Human:Guardian communications and understanding. One interesting point that came out of this was the fact that Red was 250 years old. Jane was 15, but mature for her age.

Gold and Adam discovered a common outlook and philosophy that lead to hours of cross discussion and analysis of many subjects; soul mates it seemed are not confined to Human:Human relationships. Gold, he discovered, was 101 years old, quite a youngster it seemed, considering they lived on average to 750 years - and we are speaking Earth years! As a point of interest, the Bible states Noah of "Ark" fame as being 950 years old. Come to think of it he had a lot in common with the Guardians, purely coincidental, or is it?

The Guardians loaded the animals by means of a cruiser, some had died from the trauma of the event as even Guardian technology could not combat psychological stress. There were humans who had been selected, by matching the database requirements for animal care and who took over the supervision of the animals with enthusiasm. Soon an understanding of the connection between database and Aura became apparent. These aliens although not infallible, knew what they were about. This realisation gave the humans confidence and respect, not to mention the determination to succeed not only for mankind but so as not to let down their rescuers. They didn't know it but this characteristic was also in the Aura database.

It finally came the turn of the last humans to depart. They were split into groups as insurance - even in the world of the Guardians accidents were not unknown, and this was a precious cargo. They were all now on the artificial asteroid, and a new era was about to begin.

The great Mothership dwarfing the artificial asteroid slowly and silently moved away. A noise, not unlike a whale's song, suddenly shattered the silence. This was emitted by the speakers on board as sound, of course, cannot be heard through space.

"A salute to you from the Mothership," explained Gold.

"Can we return it?" said Adam?

"Of course," said Gold. He then signalled to Red who reached out to the wall with the result that a similar sound was emitted in reply.

A fight for survival of the human race was about to begin, assisted by two selfless Guardians, like keepers of the light-house, isolated by a storm.

Chapter 17

In the years that followed the human survivors and the Guardians became great friends and learned from each other, although it must be said that the humans learnt more from the Guardians. There was every expertise required to build up a society of decent, hard working and considerate people; there was work for everyone.

The selection system that the Guardians used proved to be very effective, with a slot for everyone and no square pegs in round holes. Research on plant systems and trees in particular was of course given priority. It was discovered, 5 years later, that the trigger for the trees was a time mechanism, which could be shortened or extended by the prevailing environmental conditions. Eventual triggering however was inevitable as long as oxygen-breathing creatures existed. Thus balancing the requirements of nature. Nature was aware, it seemed, that if oxygen-breathing creatures became too widespread they would win space at the expense of the vegetation. Then the outcome would be the death of all, leaving a barren, oxygen depleted planet. A desert not unlike Mars.

Did it take the death of Mars, Adam wondered, for the trees to learn this lesson? Were they now equipped to maintain the life of a planet regardless of the ignorance of the oxygen breathers who thought it was theirs to inherit and destroy for their own immediate selfish aims? We could learn a lot from trees, he thought, if we listen to them, like the Guardians, rather than talking to them as we do, as fools. The trouble is that all we seem to say is 'get out of the way I need your flesh and the space you take'. Now we know their bite is worse than their bark. (Sorry!) Will we learn, as they appear to have done? Or will we go the way of the dinosaurs or possibly the Martians? If Adam and his fellow survivors were successful maybe they will be given another shot at it.

Jenny touched his shoulder. "A penny for your thoughts," she said. Both recalled that evening in September now a long time ago and on another world.

"Still dreaming sweetheart," he replied.

The years rolled on and everyone attained an expertise of some sort and grew accustomed and familiar with the new surroundings. Some had difficulty in believing that they would never see Earth again, but things here were much to their liking and they had videos of old Earth and they were holographic. It was almost as good as being there except that they knew in their minds that they were not. Have you ever noticed how much more exciting live television is compared with a video recording? People would get up at 3.30 am to catch a Grand Prix or a World Title Fight, even though they had video recorders. Then again, the "real thing" with the complete atmosphere, even though it cost hundreds of pounds, with a much reduced view and coverage of the event, was still found to be better. The same feel was also missing from these experiences, and somewhere deep in their souls they longed to smell the grass and feel the wind and natural warmth of the sun and know they were the people of Earth.

Much was achieved in the understanding between the two species and Adam felt in a way that mankind had been brought down a peg or two, to a better understanding of his own position. If he had learned that he was not the supreme creation that he thought himself to be, maybe it would be a good thing in the long term, for all.

Adam died 20 years later, and as he entered the final dream of death he was happy to have experienced the friendship of a superior lifeform - seemingly what he had been born for. His body was slipped into space to travel forever in the vastness of the Universe. A window was made in the coffin lid precisely to his requirements, as he had made it himself, and although the coffin was synthetic it was remarkably similar to mahogany.

Jenny touched it as she had touched the first piece of furniture Adam ever made for her and she remembered that warm natural friendly texture of the real thing. Maybe the love that went into it could be felt, as though stored in the wood like some storage battery of nature. Why then had the trees turned on man she thought? Maybe they were being cruel to be kind, God alone knows and only time will tell.

Adam knew, he had figured it out along with his friend Gold. They were satisfied that God knew what he was doing and all would be right in the universe as long as the Devil was kept at bay. The problem and solution were one and the same - recognition. The problem is not to recognise the impostor and the solution is to do so, and to act, however drastic the measures, so long as they are right. The quicker the action the less drastic the measures. Sometimes the Devil wins - sometimes he is defeated. The battle is constant and a part of life, for without the Devil and evil, God and Good are not possible. As positive requires a negative, as up needs down, as in needs out. One cannot exist without the other; there must be a comparative measure. Bearing this in mind the evil and destructive things that have happened and will continue to happen are understandable and must not be blamed on God or provide argument for his non-existence, but must be squarely placed where they belong on the shoulders of the Devil. For they need each other and cannot exist independently, but mix like matter and anti-matter, not at all!

This is but one fictitious scenario. Maybe you know better? Then tell someone! Or maybe you just scoff and live for today and yourself, and the Devil take tomorrow?

Chapter 18

The years passed and the population expanded to 5024. Although they seemed to be adapted to this lifestyle - after all they had never seen Earth - they felt that something was missing and they felt a need to return to their roots. That desire never faded, through the generations, as they experienced the old days through holographics.

The number of 5024 was never exceeded and the population started to decline. No alarm bells rang until they found that the classroom space that they had continually needed to enlarge, were found to be less full and teachers had lower pupil:teacher ratios.

The teachers raised the alarm, and the researchers found that the sperm count was reducing. They forecast that at that rate of decline, in 50 years time, the males would be sterile. It was found that this was also the case with the animals. In fact the situation here was worse, they had struggled to keep the numbers that they started with. This had been put down to the environmental change, that they were well aware of, as having a detrimental affect. They had discovered this on Earth - or rather their ancestors had - over 500 years before. This was how long it had been since they left Earth.

Experiments were urgently required and answers found if they were to survive beyond the generations produced in the next half century. The human race faced extinction once more.

The problem was not overcome in the following 50 years but a delaying solution was devised with the help of the Guardians. The ageing process was slowed and people were expected to live longer, not as long as the Guardians but 500 years was thought possible. This proved to be correct.

It was 1000 years AEE (After Earth Evacuation) when an expedition to Earth discovered that the brown covering of dust had receded to the landmasses, the predominant colour was blue again with white cloud, but the land was still covered in the brown dust. Tests showed that the toxicity of the dust had decayed, as all natural things tend to do, and was near to being harmless to humans or other oxygen breathers. The trees had reverted to producing oxygen and the dust was as a fertiliser so that they now flourished more than ever. The test indicated that 200 more years would clear the Earth of all toxic dust, by natural erosion

The problem of reproduction had not yet been overcome, but there was hope from an unexpected source. Experimentation had shown that a hybrid foetus could be produced, a hybrid Guardian:Human. Genetic material was taken from the human male ribs and a Guardian male sperm, enabling artificial insemination into a female human to create a human male capable of living for a much longer period, or so the theory suggested. The development was thwarted many times as the offspring had fatal genetic defects. Some hybrids survived for a short time as it was not considered morally justifiable to terminate them simply because they were imperfect. They were not however capable of restarting human life, as was the original aim.

A basically humanoid male and female were sought and the Guardian side was too strong for the purpose. After many years of experimentation and failure the hybrid experiment was discontinued. The experiment was meant to be however, although some argued that it was not, it was against nature and doomed to failure. The irony was that one of the hybrids that survived eventually solved the problem.

This hybrid was a female, nicknamed Goldy because of her hair colour, although some said it was because of her genetic connection with Gold - of founding father fame. Both were appropriate names, although Guardians were bald, she being a hybrid was not hairless and she did have genetic connection to Gold. She was however infertile, one of the problems encountered with the project. Her compensation however was a brilliant mind, she possessed the attributes of both races, which the combination seemed to enhance, and she worked tirelessly to solve the dilemma that the human race now found itself in.

Goldy was sent on a field research trip to Earth in the year 1180 AEE. The air was now breathable, the humans still required breathing equipment, due to the low oxygen content but because of her Guardian connection, she required less oxygen than a human and did not need the breathing apparatus. There were 12 in the expedition, the tradition continued, and six had been landed to research the scene. The dust it was found had decomposed everything of the humans and no trace was left. Even the buildings had eroded at an accelerated rate due to the dust's effects and nothing remained to show for man's years on Earth.

To say nothing was left was not entirely true, for there was one aspect of man's creativity, or organisation may be a more accurate word. They found gardens that, although grown wild, were still recognisable as organised plantation. The beauty was such an astounding mixture of cultivated and natural, that it took their breath away. The deadly dust that had killed so many was a natural fertiliser to the plants.

The humans that remained and made up this team were now quite elderly even for their extended life span. One such kindly man commented that the mixture of cultivated and natural beauty produced here was matched only by Eden's beauty, brought about by a mixture of the two races. Eden, by the way, was the real name of the hybrid female, taken from their historic recordings of the collectors Eddy and Doreen, all five where remembered with great respect and reverence along with the other collectors. 'Ed' for Eddy and 'en' from the end of Doreen.

She preferred Goldy. "Chivalry is not dead in the human breast, thank you kind sir" she replied with a smile. She picked a rose and added it to her collection of plant and soil samples. Later in the laboratory of the cruiser, Eden made a startling discovery that was to give the humans hope.

The soil samples displayed something extra to the samples taken before the evacuation (these records being stored in their computer database). These new samples showed the traces of dust from the poison. This was not a surprise but what was surprising, was the fact that the poison had eroded and had become a fertiliser which they already had determined was very effective on the plants.

The major find however, which Eden made through many hours of study and inspiration from somewhere she described simply as 'above', was that the fertiliser was not only effective on plants but also on humans. It contained condensed eroded human remains in great concentration from some sites, presumably the cities and other largely populated areas. All was not simply dust but highly potent dust containing blood, bonemeal, salts, and other concentrations of bodily concentrate. The effect of the poison had converted the remains, in addition to its own conversion, in a similar way to the compost produced as rotting matter - even of sewage materials - is rotted down on the old compost heaps. This resulting dust was thus converted into a universal fertiliser that brought a new meaning to the term, the fertile earth. Eden had extracted the necessary essence after tests in her lab. After many failures she finally tested a successful culture, and succeeded in fertilising a human egg using human sperm that was activated by the extracted culture.

Great interest was taken in the development of the embryo as you can imagine, but there was no reason to suspect that, once fertilised and developing, all would not be satisfactory. This was a worrying if exciting time. Eden had not yet shared the news with the people. Although her fellow scientists and gynaecologists were all involved and fascinated, the suspense was unbelievable.

Adny, her colleague and friend, wanted to announce Eden's success - but Eden would have none of it until a child was born successfully. Adny was a human woman of 50 years of age, which was young by their present standards. You may have figured out the derivation of her name- Adam and Jenny of course. Another revered couple, even after 1200 years.

Amy Jones had a statue in the hall of memories and Jane Briant was eventually elected to the governing body with responsibility for education. She married a communications engineer, had 3 children and died at the age of 95. Having honed her telepathic talents to an extremely high standard, under the guidance of Red, she finished her working days as a councillor to troubled minds. Her contribution to the healing and soothing of the mentally and spiritually disturbed, of which there were many in the early days, was recognised by an award and more importantly by the love and affection of all she met and many she didn't. Red was 700 years old when he died and the last words he was heard to whisper were.. "Janey I hear...." and he raised his hand of four fingers which observers swear appeared to grasp and interlap with an invisible hand of five fingers that depressed the flesh where the fingers touched inside and out on both sides of his four. There was also a strong scent of violets, the flower that Jane used to prefer and always had on her dressing table, teachers table and councillor's quarters.

You may recall the family of three, the father of which was stopped by the collectors. He, his wife explained, had beaten them both in drunken bouts of ill-tempered abuse. His son still missed him terribly.

And the vagrant with the medals? Well, it transpired that Tom, for that was his name, had saved his whole group of seven in North Africa by distracting a Panzer tank, which had discovered their location in the wadi where they were sleeping. He was the lookout who heard their approach and being well educated could speak German. To wake his group would have meant immediate attack and obvious annihilation, as the heaviest weapons they possessed were their rifles. With lightening wit he threw off his uniform and rushed out yelling in German that they were all German and "don't fire". All the German eyes were on the near naked single man shouting in German. Confusion reigned and in the confusion the British slipped into the darkness and escaped. A few shells burst out in their direction but they had been given the vital minutes to scatter and slip away in various directions.

The Germans shot Tom when they discovered his British clothes and rifle and left him for dead in the desert. They shot him through the head with a single shot, but miraculously he lived and was picked up by a patrol the same night after the

Germans left. It was a miracle the fact that his brain was not fatally damaged, the bullet had gone under the brain through his neck and throat and taken a piece out of a vertebra. Tom was awarded a VC, which they thought would be posthumous, but this man had God on his side. His fellow man however was not. He was never the same again and unable to find work after the war he deteriorated into vagrancy.

The selection database had been justified in its choice when 3 years after his collection a small boy who had been climbing a gantry, for the hell of it, slipped and fell. Tom saw the boy and was making his way towards him when he fell. Without hesitation Tom positioned himself under the boy with no hope of catching him, for the boy was 5 years old and falling from 10 metres high. Tom knew perfectly well what he was doing as the boy hit him in the chest and broke his fall. As they both went down Tom's weakened spine was broken instantly. The boy fractured his pelvis and right arm, but lived to become a scout-ship pilot. Tom died the hero he always was.

The Guardians could not understand how he had been abandoned by society for most of his life. The humans had no reply! He was buried with military honours or as near as they could make it, and his medals, including his VC, were displayed in the memorial hall. The boy, come pilot, visited the hall each birthday until he too died aged 90 years.

Not forgetting Charley, he lived longer than any dog on Earth and left a strong line of pups to carry on his ancestry. He never did get used to the new environment, to ride on a levitation board was never quite the same as the smell of the air blowing passed his face as he sat on the back of Adam's pickup.

Jane had said how she sensed that he also missed the timber. This was something they all missed but perhaps for different reasons. A friend turned foe unexpectedly was always hard to take. But does the end justify the means? We will have to wait and see!

Chapter 19

The child was born in the laboratory, from the dust of Earth you could say. To everyone's delight he cried on cue and had all the right parts in the right places and a brain scan showed potentially normal development capacity.

Eden was now ready to declare her discovery and creation; she would not however allow it to be referred to as a creation of hers. She insisted that only through the grace of God had she discovered one of nature's solutions to one of nature's problems.

In recognition of her work and achievement, the garden-like area of Earth, which they discovered and from which they took the dust sample, was named after her. The problems were far from over as the newly born required a mate to restart the human race and they needed the Earth's environment to stay fertile. The boy grew into a youth and there was no young female to accompany him. But Eden was also working on this problem and as their most proven method of cloning and genetic reproduction was material from the ribs, this is where she started her research. Her objective was to produce a female compatible with her first success. Adny again worked alongside her on the new project. Speed, once more, being of the essence.

The boy was becoming a man. The time had come for him to be transferred to Earth in order to maintain his fertility, and for him to become accustomed to the environment. It was now the year 1200 AEE and the Guardians felt it appropriate to restart the calendar for the humans and therefore the day the boy/man was placed on Earth was given the date year 1 ET (Eden Time).

In the year 3 ET a female was taken to join him. The reinstatement of the human race had begun and Armageddon was yet to come. The last words were to warn of the possibility that the fruit of certain trees may still be affected. Don't touch the fruit of such trees! But that is another story.

The outpost in the asteroids continued to monitor the progress of mankind for 12 years. With God's help they had managed to prevent their extinction, or maybe it was they who were helping God.

It was in the year 1212 AEE by local asteroid time when the Mothership Atlantis received an emergency alarm and responded as soon as she could. She was three months distant and the alarm was brief and vague. "We are being taken up, but we have no fear."

When the Atlantis reached their destination no trace of the artificial world was found. They did find a simulated mahogany coffin with the name 'Adam Briant' and a simple 'In Memoriam, Dreamer'.

The coffin was empty but no sign of any interference was found. It remained a mystery; maybe it was the reason for the camouflage; had some malevolent alien taken them? Being 'taken up' however - a strange comment in the circumstances. Which way is up in space? Could they have meant to a higher plane of existence? I hope so, don't you?

A circle has no end, and no beginning only a path to where it originated. You have arrived no matter where you are, as long as you stay on the path.